"Jessica," Elizabeth said between giggles, "let me get this straight. We were each pretending to be each other—"

"—just so we could be with the guy we really liked!" Jessica finished the sentence, and they both collapsed with laughter.

Elizabeth's forehead wrinkled with concern. "How do we tell them without hurting their feelings?"

"Good point," Jessica said, sighing heavily. "I can't just tell Chris I'd rather be with Nick and you can't just tell Nick you'd rather be with Chris."

"What are we going to do?" Elizabeth moaned as she flopped down beside Jessica.

Jessica thought about it for a few minutes. Then she bolted up. "I've got it!" she exclaimed.

"What?" Elizabeth asked, raising herself up onto her elbows.

"I don't know about you, but I had Nick totally convinced I was you," Jessica informed her sister.

A slow smile spread across Elizabeth's face. "And I had Chris totally convinced I was you!" she added, sitting all the way up.

"Are you thinking what I'm thinking?" Jessica asked, her eyes twinkling with excitement.

Elizabeth nodded. "Let's switch places for the rest of the trip."

SWEET VALLEY TWINS

Twins in Love

Written by
Jamie Suzanne

Created by
FRANCINE PASCAL

BANTAM BOOKS
NEW YORK · TORONTO · LONDON · SYDNEY · AUCKLAND

To Anna-Lily Chase

RL 4, 008-012

TWINS IN LOVE
A Bantam Book / November 1996

Sweet Valley High® and Sweet Valley Twins® are
registered trademarks of Francine Pascal.

Conceived by Francine Pascal.

Produced by Daniel Weiss Associates, Inc.
33 West 17th Street
New York, NY 10011.

Cover art by James Mathewuse.

ISBN: 0-553-48346-3

Published simultaneously in the United States and Canada

Bantam Books are published by Bantam Books, a division of Bantam
Doubleday Dell Publishing Group, Inc. Its trademark, consisting of the
words "Bantam Books" and the portrayal of a rooster, is Registered in the
U.S. Patent and Trademark Office and in other countries. Marca
Registrada. Bantam Books, 1540 Broadway, New York, New York 10036.

PRINTED IN THE UNITED STATES OF AMERICA

OPM   0 9 8 7 6 5 4 3 2 1

One

◇

"Come on, Lila, please!" Jessica Wakefield begged. "*Please* let me borrow one of your cowboy hats for my trip on Monday." She had one of Lila's hats on her head and the other two in her hands. "You're not going to wear all three of these during break."

Lila Fowler flipped her brown hair over her shoulder. "I'm not going to wear any of them during break," she admitted. "Cowboy hats aren't exactly considered high fashion in Paris. But that's not the point. They're all brand-new, Jessica. I usually like to wear my things at least once before I lend them out."

Jessica sighed as she took off the hat and tossed it in a chair. She didn't see what the big deal was. Lila would probably never wear any of these hats.

If three months from now she suddenly needed a cowboy hat, she'd say these three were out of style and go out and buy three new ones.

"I know, Lila, but I really need a cowboy hat now," Jessica pleaded. Her whole family was going to the Triple Z Ranch over winter break, and it was absolutely vital that she look her best.

Lila Fowler is the most spoiled person I've ever met, Jessica thought bitterly as she plopped down on Lila's huge bed. *She's the richest girl in Sweet Valley and she won't even share a lousy cowboy hat with her best friend.*

"Oh, all right!" Lila sighed as though she were making a huge sacrifice. "If you're going to sulk, take one of the hats."

"Really?" Jessica squealed as she sat up. She grabbed the tan hat with the fancy trim. "You'll let me borrow this?"

"It's not like I have much choice," Lila grumbled. "Just don't get it dirty."

"I won't! I promise!" Jessica hugged her friend and jumped off the bed, putting on the hat. "What do you think?" she asked, twirling around in front of Lila's full-length mirror.

Lila shrugged. "It looks good," she admitted grudgingly.

Jessica rolled her eyes. "It looks great!" she declared, admiring herself in Lila's mirror. "I'm going to have so much fun next week. There are going to be so many cute guys at the ranch and probably not very many girls. In fact, out on the open range there will probably be guys who haven't even seen a girl in months. I'll have to divide my time between the five or six cutest ones."

"What about Elizabeth?" Lila asked, folding her arms across her chest. "She'll be there, won't she?"

"Yeah, she'll be there," Jessica said with a shrug. "But come on, Lila. She'll be too busy riding horses. Besides, Elizabeth and I never go for the same kind of guy."

Elizabeth was Jessica's identical twin sister. Both girls were twelve years old and sixth-graders at Sweet Valley Middle School. They had the same long sun-streaked blond hair and blue-green eyes, and each had a dimple in her left cheek. But the two were totally different in personality.

Elizabeth was a serious student who loved reading and writing. She actually did her homework every single night. In her spare time she would read books for fun, get together with her friends, ride horses, and work on *The Sweet Valley Sixers*, the sixth-grade newspaper she helped start with her best friend, Amy Sutton.

Jessica, on the other hand, only did homework if it was absolutely necessary. If she had to read something, it was usually a fashion magazine or anything that included an article on the singer Johnny Buck. But there were usually too many other things competing for her time. Things like boys, clothes, makeup, and the Unicorn Club.

The Unicorn Club was the most important group at Sweet Valley Middle School. Not everyone was privileged enough to belong, of course. Only the most beautiful and popular girls at school were Unicorns. Jessica and Lila were both members. But Elizabeth wasn't. It wasn't that Elizabeth wasn't pretty enough or popular enough to be a Unicorn; she just chose not to be one. If Elizabeth would pass up the opportunity to belong to the most exclusive club at school, Jessica knew they'd never have to worry about liking the same guy.

That would never happen—especially *not at the Triple Z Ranch,* Jessica thought triumphantly. *Elizabeth would probably be too busy riding horses twenty-four hours a day.*

When it came to dude ranches, Jessica was definitely more into the "dude" part than the "ranch" part. Jessica didn't like horses, and they didn't like her either, so she'd have the guys all to herself without an ounce of competition from her twin sister.

"Well, you're not the only one who's going to have a fun break, Jessica," Lila informed her. "Did I tell you Daddy and I are going to spend some quality time shopping in Paris?"

Only about a hundred times, Jessica thought, frowning.

"There are plenty of cute guys in Paris too, you know," Lila went on. "And they're much better looking than American guys, not to mention more sophisticated."

"Oooh-la-la," Jessica said sarcastically. "Like your father would really let you go out with a strange guy in a foreign country."

"He would if I met a guy I really wanted to go out with," Lila insisted. "French guys are real gentlemen. They're very cultured and classy. Not like the cowboys you'll be spending time with."

Jessica scowled. Even though Lila was her best friend, she hated it when she acted like a snob. "Well, I'm planning on having a true midwinter-break romance," Jessica said. "No matter what it takes."

"Even if it means getting on a horse?" Lila asked, a hint of smugness in her voice.

Jessica paused. She really had to think about that one. "Absolutely," she replied. "Nothing's going to stop me. Not even a stupid old horse."

"Wow, Jess!" Lila exclaimed, laughing. "You really *are* determined, aren't you!"

"Can you believe it?" Elizabeth Wakefield asked Amy Sutton. "Five whole days at the Triple Z Ranch!" Elizabeth was taking her riding clothes out of her closet and hanging them on the door in preparation for packing.

Amy sank back against the pillows on Elizabeth's bed. "You are so lucky!" she cried. "You're going to have such a fun time. Maybe you can write about it for the *Sixers*."

"I know," Elizabeth replied, gazing up at her poster of the famous racehorse Man o' War. She hoped there'd be a horse that looked like him at the ranch.

"You know, I used to go riding a lot at Carson Stable," Elizabeth continued as she sat down beside Amy. "But there's just been so much going on at school these last few months that I've hardly been out there at all. I wonder if I even remember how to ride?"

"Oh, I think it'll come back to you pretty quickly," Amy said with a laugh. "I seriously doubt that you, of all people, would forget how to ride a horse."

"Yeah," Elizabeth agreed. "I can't wait to see all those beautiful horses. There will be so many to choose from. I'll want to ride them all."

"Aren't you going to spend a little time doing anything else, Elizabeth?" Amy asked. "Like checking out the local male population, maybe?"

"Oh, please, Amy!" Elizabeth said, laughing. "Jessica is going to have that ground covered, believe me. I'm just going to concentrate on the three *R*s: riding, reading, and relaxing."

"Well, while you're out there having the time of your life, think of me back here in Sweet Valley with nothing to do," Amy said with a heavy sigh.

Elizabeth felt a stab of guilt. "I'm sorry, Amy," she said softly. "I've really been going on and on, haven't I?"

Amy shrugged. "No biggie," she said, forcing a smile. "I'd probably do the same thing if it was me. You just go and have a great time."

"I will!" Elizabeth promised. "Triple Z Ranch, here I come!"

Jessica set two suitcases on the driveway beside the Wakefields' minivan on Monday morning. "I'll go get the rest of my suitcases," she said, skipping toward the house.

"The *rest* of your suitcases?" Mr. and Mrs. Wakefield asked together.

Jessica stopped. "Mom, Dad, we're going to be there for five days," she explained. "That's a long time. I have to have clothes for warm weather and cold weather, clothes for dressing up and dressing down, and clothes to match the style of any guy I might happen to meet."

"What about riding clothes?" Mrs. Wakefield teased.

"Oh, right," Jessica said, shrugging. "Those too."

A scruffy head suddenly shot out of one of the minivan's windows. It was Steven, the twins' older brother. "What's that I hear, Jessica?"

Steven could be a very cool guy every once in a

while. The twins even went to him for advice sometimes when they really needed it. But right now Steven was doing what he did best: irritating the twins. And Jessica was his current target.

"Are you *actually* going to get on a horse, Jessica?" he continued in a shocked voice. "I didn't think horses were your thing."

Jessica felt her cheeks redden, but she wasn't about to let her brother get the best of her. "For your information, Steven, I am every bit as good with horses as Elizabeth," Jessica said haughtily.

Steven snorted. "Yeah, right."

"Yeah, right!" Jessica said firmly. *As long as I don't have to do more than look at them,* she said to herself.

"Since when," Steven demanded.

"Since always," Jessica snapped. "I've just never had the chance to display my true talents." *There*, she thought. *That should keep him quiet.*

Steven smirked. "We've got five days ahead of us at the ranch," he said. "You'll have plenty of opportunities to show the world what a skilled horsewoman you are."

Not if I can help it, Jessica promised herself. *I'm going to meet a tall, dark, and handsome stranger— maybe even three or four of them—at the ranch, and then I'll have no time to even get near the horses.*

Jessica leaned against the minivan and imagined her dream vacation with her dream guy. *We'd hang out in the main lodge and watch videos,* she thought, *or maybe we'd even take a walk through the woods.*

And by the end of the week, maybe, just maybe, we'd ride off together into the sunset.

In a Porsche or something.

Two

"Wow! Look at this place!" Elizabeth drew in her breath as she stepped out of the car.

The Wakefields stood in front of a large log building that was probably the main lodge. Beyond that was a row of cabins and a hill leading down to the stables. Next to the stables was a huge pasture where dozens of horses were grazing.

They were mostly quarter horses, but Elizabeth noticed a couple of Morgans as well. There were bays, buckskins, chestnuts—horses of all colors and markings. *It's a good thing people at these ranches decide which horse you should ride*, Elizabeth thought. *I don't think I could ever choose which one I liked best.*

"This is like a dream come true," Elizabeth said. "It's beautiful."

"Come on, Elizabeth," Mrs. Wakefield called.

"You can go down and see the horses in a little bit. But right now we should get checked in."

Elizabeth grinned. "OK," she said reluctantly, dragging herself back to her family.

Jessica glanced around her. "I wonder where the cowboys are?"

Elizabeth pursed her lips. "Are you here to ride horses or ogle guys, Jess?" she asked affectionately.

"I'm *definitely* here to ogle guys," Jessica replied with a grin.

"Hello!" a strange voice bellowed. "And welcome to the Triple Z Ranch!" A tall, husky man with graying hair came out of the lodge. He was followed by a short, thin woman who wore her red hair in a thick braid down her back. The couple looked a little older than Elizabeth's parents. They wore matching Triple Z Ranch T-shirts.

The man held out his right hand to Mr. Wakefield. "I'm Carl Hogan," he said with a big smile. "And this is my wife, Maddie."

"Pleased to meet you," Mrs. Hogan put in. A gold crown sparkled on her front tooth when she smiled.

Mr. Wakefield returned their handshakes. "I'm Ned Wakefield. This is my wife, Alice, and our children, Steven, Jessica, and Elizabeth," he introduced them.

"Hello, Steven," Mr. Hogan said. He turned to the twins and did a double take. So did his wife.

"Oh, my goodness!" Mrs. Hogan exclaimed,

bringing her hands to her cheeks and glancing from one twin to the other. "Look at you! You two look exactly alike!"

Elizabeth glanced sideways at her twin.

Jessica rolled her eyes in response.

"They're twins, Maddie," Mr. Hogan said with a wide smile.

"Twins!" Mrs. Hogan cried as though she'd never heard the word before. "Amazing. And so cute too. Land sakes, how will we ever tell you two apart?"

"We could tattoo a big black *J* on Jessica's forehead and a big black *E* on Elizabeth's forehead," Steven suggested.

"*Steven.*" Mrs. Wakefield shot him a warning look.

"Or we could just give them plain old name tags," Mrs. Hogan replied, winking at Jessica.

Name tags! Jessica thought indignantly. "You don't need name tags to tell us apart," she said politely. "You see, I always wear my hair long and Elizabeth always wears hers pulled back."

"That's right." Elizabeth nodded.

Mrs. Hogan didn't look convinced. "That's too easy," she declared with a wave of her hand. "You two could get up in the morning and just switch hairstyles and no one would be the wiser."

"That only happens in the movies, Mrs. Hogan," Jessica said, winking at Elizabeth.

"Enough introductions," Mr. Hogan blustered. "Let's head into the lodge for a grand tour, shall we?" He waved the Wakefields through the lodge entrance.

"Whoa! Check this out!" Steven exclaimed when they got inside.

The main room was like a large family room. The log walls were covered with elk, bear, and bison heads.

"I've never seen so many animal heads in one room before," Steven said, awestruck.

"Yuck," Jessica said, turning away in disgust. She noticed a small gift shop in the corner and breathed a sigh of relief. "Hey, Elizabeth, look!" Jessica pointed at the gift shop and stared at it as if it were an oasis in the middle of a desert.

"All right!" Elizabeth put in. "We can buy postcards and Triple Z Ranch shirts."

"That's right, ladies." Mr. Hogan smiled at them. "The shop is open from ten until six every day. Feel free to stop in anytime."

Steven rolled his eyes. "Can't you two go anywhere without thinking about shopping?" he griped.

Mr. Hogan laughed and hooked his thumbs in his belt loops. "Welcome to the lodge," he explained. "This is our main room. People come here to relax after a hard day's ride."

There were lots of comfy-looking chairs and sofas scattered throughout the room. A cozy fire burned in the corner fireplace.

"This looks like a nice place to hang out," Steven said.

"There are all kinds of games in there." Mr. Hogan nodded toward a row of cabinets that lined the east wall. "Monopoly, Parcheesi, whatever you like. Just help yourselves."

"Where's the TV and VCR?" Jessica asked, looking around frantically.

"Oh, we don't have 'em." Mr. Hogan shook his head. "We figure you city folk come out here to get away from it all."

"That's for sure." Mr. Wakefield nodded.

"Yeah, but we don't come to get away from TV!" Jessica said, frowning. *What kind of place doesn't have a TV?* she wondered. "What if something really important happens while we're here? Like what if Johnny Buck gets married or something?"

"That's not too likely," Elizabeth reassured her sister.

"But it's *possible*. And we wouldn't find out about it until we got back to Sweet Valley!"

"Chill out, Jessica." Steven groaned. "You'll survive a few days without TV. Let's concentrate on the really important things, like *where do we eat?*"

"The dining hall is right this way," Mr. Hogan said, leading them through the main room and into a large room with lots of tables. Three of the walls were paneled. The fourth was lined with floor-to-ceiling windows and glass doors that led to a huge deck.

"Wow! What a view!" Elizabeth exclaimed, rushing over to the windows.

Jessica followed her over. "You're telling me," she remarked when she noticed the stable hands down below. "Nature never looked so good."

The dining hall overlooked the stables and the horse-filled pasture. Riding instructors, stable hands, and cowboys could be seen making their rounds. In the distance the Sierra Nevada rose, creating a picture-postcard scene.

"This is where you'll take most of your meals," Mr. Hogan told them. "If you care for something in between, you'll see we have several vending machines. And we always have a pot of coffee on." He pointed to the counter at the front of the room.

Mr. Hogan slid open one of the glass doors and gestured for the Wakefields to follow him out onto the deck. "You can see some of our horses down there."

"How many horses do you have here, Mr. Hogan?" Elizabeth asked, gazing down at the pasture.

"About fifty. And they're all very good, gentle horses. You don't have to worry about any of them running away with you."

"You mean they're all slow?" Steven moaned.

Mr. Hogan glanced at Steven. "Oh, no," he said. "We've got a few livelier ones. If you're an experienced rider, talk to Andrew Hillestad down there. Andrew's the one in the red-checkered shirt."

"Mmm, he's cute," Jessica said, resting her chin in her hand as she leaned over the railing.

"They're *all* cute to you, Jess," Elizabeth teased, nudging her twin sister.

"They're all cute, period," Jessica responded, waving at a cowboy who was passing by. He tipped his hat in response, and the twins collapsed into giggles.

"Andrew's the one who assigns all the horses," Mr. Hogan went on. "He can set you up with an animal that has a little fire."

"Great," Steven said.

"You know we have a friendly little race on the last day. The winner gets a genuine Triple Z cowboy hat not unlike the one your little sister here is wearing," Mr. Hogan said, giving Jessica's hat a pat. "If you've had some experience riding, you might consider entering."

"I certainly will," Steven said enthusiastically.

"You!" Jessica and Elizabeth squawked at the same time.

"You don't know anything about riding, Steven," Elizabeth said, laughing.

Steven cleared his throat. "I know enough," he said.

"Enough to get yourself thrown in a mud puddle," Jessica muttered.

"Now, girls. Don't go giving your brother a hard time," Mr. Hogan said. He looked at them both harder. "Which one of you wears the long hair again?"

"Jessica," Elizabeth said.

"Elizabeth," Jessica said at the same time.

Mr. Hogan laughed. "I'll have to keep an eye on you two," he said as he turned back into the lodge.

Steven rolled his eyes. "I'm surprised he didn't pinch your cheeks and tell you all about how cute you are."

"Come on, Steven," Elizabeth said. "We can't help being twins."

Steven sighed. "No matter where we go, you guys get all the attention. Just because you're twins. Big deal! You're not the only set of twins on the planet, you know."

"We know," Jessica said. "But it looks like we're the only set of twins here." She turned to Elizabeth. "Let's go check out our cabin, OK?"

"OK," Elizabeth said, running into the lodge with her sister.

"Just you watch me," Steven yelled after the twins. "I'm going to win the race *and* the cowboy hat. You'll see!"

"Cute guys," Jessica said appreciatively as she closed the door to her and Elizabeth's room.

The log cabin they were staying in had three rooms. Mr. and Mrs. Wakefield had the largest one, and Steven had the smallest. The twins had the one in-between.

"Nice horses," Elizabeth responded.

"Guys!"

"Horses!"

"Guys!"

Elizabeth wrinkled her nose at her sister. "I'll take a horse over a guy any day," she declared.

Jessica snorted as she unzipped one of her suitcases. "You would. Really, Lizzie. You need to get out more!"

Elizabeth laughed. "I get out plenty," she replied as she took neat stacks of clothing out of her suitcase and placed them on her bed.

Jessica went to the closet to grab some hangers. "Oh, my gosh!" she gasped.

"What?" Elizabeth glanced up.

"Would you believe there are only four hangers in here?"

Elizabeth let out her breath. "Jessica," she said patiently. "Four hangers is not a crisis."

"It is when there are two of us sharing this closet. Do the math, Elizabeth. Two of us plus five days does not equal four hangers!"

Elizabeth sighed. "Leave me one for my dress and you can have the other three," she said. "I can use the bureau."

"Thanks, but that doesn't help much," Jessica said as she stared forlornly into the closet. "I know we're supposed to be roughing it, but this is unreal."

Elizabeth opened the bottom bureau drawer

and set a stack of jeans inside. "Why'd you bring so much stuff anyway?" she asked. "All you really need are jeans and one dress for a fancy dinner."

Jessica sighed. *Elizabeth may be a brilliant student*, she thought, *but clothing is a subject she needs to study a little more.* "I like to look my best, OK?" she said, tossing her hair over her shoulder.

"Just in case the ranch hosts an impromptu fashion show?" Elizabeth teased. She closed the bureau and headed for the door.

Jessica frowned. "Hey, where are you going?" she asked. "Do you have all your stuff put away already?"

"Yup," Elizabeth said over her shoulder. "I'm going to go get fitted for boots. If I get fitted now, maybe I'll have time to get in a quick ride before dinner."

"Is that all you're going to do while we're here?" Jessica asked, hands on her hips. "Ride horses?"

"That *is* why we're here, Jess," Elizabeth said, closing the door on her way out.

"Maybe that's why *you're* here," Jessica muttered. She turned to her suitcases and pulled out one of her newer outfits. "Now, let's see," she said to herself. "Do I have time to get in some quick guy watching before dinner?"

Elizabeth chose a pair of plain black cowboy boots from the shelf in the barn. She slid them on, then stood up. "Ow," she moaned as her toes squished together. "Too tight."

She took those off, returned them to the shelf, and chose another pair. Black with white rhinestones this time. *These are more Jessica's style,* she thought, sliding them on anyway. Better. But still too tight.

I'm never *going to get to go riding,* Elizabeth thought desperately.

"Well, hello there," came a voice behind her.

Elizabeth turned, startled. There in the doorway stood the cutest boy she'd ever seen.

He looked about thirteen. He was a little taller than Elizabeth, and he had dark wavy hair and gorgeous green eyes.

Elizabeth felt her cheeks flush. *What amazing eyes,* she thought. She couldn't find a thing to say.

"B-B-Boots," she finally stammered. "I'm, uh, looking for some." She replaced the black boots with the white rhinestones and pulled out another pair. Any pair. Just so it looked like she would rather try on boots than stare at this cute guy.

Which, she realized with surprise, she didn't.

The boy flashed her a smile that lit up his whole face. "Just checking out the stables," he said with a wave. "I'll see you around."

And then he was gone.

Elizabeth hurried to the door. The boy was already over by the pasture. A light breeze rippled through his hair as he stood leaning against the fence, seemingly lost in his own thoughts.

Elizabeth's heart pounded as she watched him. She could tell he was different from most boys she knew. There was something special about him. *There's probably no one else like him in the world,* she thought. *No other guy could possibly be that cute.*

"I hope I'll see you around," she whispered. But then she shook her head. *I'm acting like Jessica,* she realized with a start. *I'm not here to meet guys,* she reminded herself. *I'm here to ride.* And with that she turned back to the wall of boots, shaking the boy from her mind.

Jessica was starving. She hoped the food was good in this place. But supper, as it was called here, wasn't for another two hours. She couldn't wait that long.

She quickly ran a brush through her hair, grabbed her purse, and headed for the vending machines in the dining hall.

As she stepped out of her cabin she noticed someone coming out of the cabin next door. It was a boy about her age, maybe a little older. He noticed Jessica just about the same time she noticed him. Their eyes met and held.

"Hello," the boy said, waving to Jessica. He was a little taller than she, with dark wavy hair and gorgeous green eyes.

Jessica flipped her hair over her shoulder. She was glad she'd taken the time to brush it before leaving her cabin.

"Hi," she replied, wiping her sweaty palms on her pants. She wished she could think of something else to say, but her stomach was tied up in knots. This guy was totally cute! And she could tell by the way he was smiling at her that he thought she was cute too. She'd seen that look before—usually on TV.

This is it, Jessica thought. *This is the boy I'm going to have my winter-break romance with.* She smiled. *Maybe it'll go beyond winter break. Maybe this is the boy I'll spend the rest of my life with.*

The boy scratched his nose. "So, uh, do you like it here at the ranch?" he asked casually.

"Uh-huh," Jessica answered as though she were in a trance.

"How long are you staying?" he asked, running a hand through his dark curly hair.

Jessica's heart was pounding so hard, she thought it might explode. "Uh, t-t-till Friday," she replied.

"Good! So are we." The boy smiled, revealing a set of perfectly straight teeth. "I'll see you around, then."

The boy took off in the direction of the lodge. Jessica just stood there and watched him go.

Jessica suddenly thought of Lila, who was on

her way to Paris. *Lila probably hasn't even gotten off the plane yet, and I've already met the cutest boy on the planet*, she realized with satisfaction.

What's happening to me? Jessica asked herself. *I've never felt like this before.* But she'd watched enough soap operas to know what it was.

I'm in love, she said to herself. *I, Jessica Wakefield, have fallen in love!*

Three

◇

"Are you Mr. Hillestad?" Steven asked a guy in a red-checkered shirt as he entered the stable.

"Sure am." The guy tipped his hat to Steven. "What can I do for you?"

"Mr. Hogan told me you could set me up with the fastest horse you've got," Steven said, glancing at the black mare that Mr. Hillestad was brushing.

"Oh, yeah." Mr. Hillestad nodded knowingly. "You're the brother of those twins, aren't you?"

Steven winced. "Yeah," he admitted grudgingly.

Mr. Hillestad grinned. "Carl was telling me about you. None of the horses have been assigned yet. But if you're really an experienced rider, I could give you a horse like Queenie here," he said, patting the black mare.

Queenie whinnied when she heard her name.

"Oh, yeah, I'm experienced," Steven assured Mr. Hillestad. *Experienced enough,* he thought. All he needed was a horse that could go. He'd just hang on. And together they'd win the race on Friday. "Do you think I could try her out right now?" Steven asked eagerly.

"Sorry." Mr. Hillestad shook his head. "We're not supposed to send any of the guests out alone. At least not on the first day. But you could walk her out to the pasture if you want. Get to know her a little bit."

"Sure," Steven said, reaching up to rub the star on Queenie's forehead.

The horse nickered in response.

Mr. Hillestad snapped a lead rope onto her bridle. "There you go," he said, handing the rope to Steven.

As Steven headed out toward the pasture an older guy was just coming in. His jeans and boots were caked with mud. He had a smudge of dirt on his face. But he was grinning from ear to ear.

"You're in a good mood, Bill," Mr. Hillestad said to the older guy.

"Yeah." The man named Bill scratched his head as Steven passed him. "I was just givin' old Rocket her bath and rememberin' the old days."

"You mean when she ran in the California Derby?" Mr. Hillestad asked.

The California Derby! Steven stopped in his tracks. *One of the horses here ran in the California Derby?*

"Those were good times, my friend," Bill said. "Too bad you're too young to remember."

Steven dropped Queenie's lead. "Excuse me," he said. He could feel the excitement building within him. "This horse you're talking about? Did she really run in the California Derby?"

Mr. Hillestad glanced at Bill. "Well—" he began.

"She sure did," Bill interrupted. "She racked up quite a few trophies in her day."

"Well, where is she?" Steven asked, looking around. "Could I see her?"

"She's tied up around the other side of the barn," Bill said. "But—"

Steven didn't wait around to hear what else Bill had to say. He had to see this horse. Even more important, he had to convince Mr. Hillestad to let him ride her.

Elizabeth sighed as she clasped her book to her chest. *Without a doubt,* Wuthering Heights *is the most romantic book ever written,* she thought. Elizabeth had already read it six times.

To Elizabeth, it wasn't just a love story. No, Catherine and Heathcliff's love was special. It was the kind of love that lasted longer than life itself. The kind of love Elizabeth hoped to find herself one day. Maybe even with that boy she saw in the barn.

Elizabeth sighed again as she imagined herself as Catherine and the boy from the barn, whatever his name was, as Heathcliff. She pictured them strolling arm in arm over the desolate moors, pledging their undying love to each other.

"What are you mooning about over there?" Jessica asked with annoyance. She was sitting cross-legged on the bed across from Elizabeth's and reading a fashion magazine.

Elizabeth turned to her sister. "Jess," she said softly and haltingly. "You're not going to believe this. I can hardly believe it myself, but—"

"What, Lizzie? Tell me!" Jessica begged, her eyes wide.

Elizabeth's heart pounded as she remembered the boy from the barn. "I—I think I may have met a boy I could like more than a horse."

"No way!" Jessica exclaimed, jumping over onto Elizabeth's bed. She threw her magazine aside. "Who is he?"

Elizabeth set her book facedown and hugged her knees to her chest. "Well, I met him earlier today, down in the barn."

"Love at first sight?" Jessica asked hopefully.

Elizabeth nodded. "I think so. I mean, when I saw him, I could hardly talk. My palms were sweating and my knees were shaking."

Jessica squealed with delight. "That sounds like love all right," she declared. "Tell me about him. What does he look like?"

"Well," Elizabeth said thoughtfully, closing her

eyes to get a clear mental picture of him. She smiled as he came into view. "He's really cute. I think he's about thirteen—"

"Yeah, what else?" Jessica asked eagerly, bouncing on the bed and waving her hand for Elizabeth to go on.

"He's a little taller than I am—"

"Tall is good," Jessica approved. "So many boys our age are shorter than we are. That's so embarrassing!"

"He's got dark wavy hair—"

Jessica's smile faded.

"—and gorgeous green eyes—"

Jessica's smile disappeared. "Which cabin is he staying in?" she demanded.

"I don't know," Elizabeth replied. "He didn't tell me. But Jess, when he left, he waved and said, 'See you around,' like he really wanted to see me again."

Jessica suddenly jumped up and stomped to the door.

"Jessica?" Elizabeth asked, her forehead wrinkled in confusion. "Where are you going?"

Slam!

Jessica heard her twin calling her, but she kept right on going. Out of the room. And out of the cabin. She had to get away from Elizabeth.

The sun was just slipping below the mountains in the distance. But Jessica was too upset to notice how pretty the sunset was. There was only one thought going through her head.

The guy with the dark wavy hair is the love of my *life, not Elizabeth's.*

"Jessica! Jessica, wait!" Elizabeth's voice was getting closer now; she was probably catching up. Jessica kept stomping forward, not caring where she was going.

Suddenly she felt a hand on her arm. "Jessica! What's the matter with you?" Elizabeth asked, out of breath.

Jessica glared at Elizabeth. "As if you didn't know!" she said, angrily pulling her arm out of her sister's grasp.

Elizabeth's face was totally blank. "I don't know," she insisted. "What are you so mad about? I was just telling you—" Suddenly she stopped. Her eyes grew wide. "Did you—"

"He's *mine*, Elizabeth." Jessica jammed her thumb to her chest. "You can't have him."

"You met the same guy?" Elizabeth asked softly.

Met him? Jessica thought indignantly. *Elizabeth makes it sound so—so insignificant. I've done more than meet the guy. We practically have a relationship!* "Don't you dare try to steal my boyfriend!" she snarled.

"Boyfriend?" Elizabeth raised an eyebrow.

"That's right," Jessica replied stiffly as she folded her arms across her chest.

"All right," Elizabeth said in a superior voice. "What's his name?"

"His name?" Jessica asked weakly.

"If he's your boyfriend, you must know his name," Elizabeth remarked.

"Well, we didn't exactly get around to telling each other our names," Jessica mumbled.

"Uh-huh," Elizabeth said knowingly.

Jessica frowned. "You don't have to know someone's name to know you're destined to be with him forever," she said quickly.

"No, but it's a good idea to find out his name before you go telling people he's your boyfriend," Elizabeth responded.

Jessica felt her back stiffen. "Well, if you're so smart, why don't you tell me his name," she demanded.

Elizabeth didn't answer. She just bit her lip and gazed off into the sunset.

"Ha!" Jessica cried triumphantly. "You don't know either."

Elizabeth blushed. "No, I don't," she admitted.

"So that means he's up for grabs," Jessica declared. "And I intend to grab him first thing tomorrow morning."

"Well, maybe instead of fighting over him, we should let him make the choice," Elizabeth suggested. "Let him choose which one of us he likes better."

"Fine with me," Jessica replied with a shrug. "But I have to say, I really admire your courage, Elizabeth. You and I both know you don't have a chance against me."

Elizabeth snorted. "We'll see, Jess. We'll see."

Four

Elizabeth sighed. Lopsided again. *French braiding is a lot harder than it looks,* she thought. *At least this particular style is.* Elizabeth undid her left braid and started over. She was trying to braid just the sides, like the girl on the cover of Jessica's magazine. *I wonder if that green-eyed boy will like this hairstyle,* she asked herself, gazing into the mirror and struggling with the braid.

"You've been in there for ten hours already," Jessica said, pounding on the bathroom door. "There are others of us who would like to use the bathroom too, you know."

"I'll be out in a minute," Elizabeth said with annoyance as she stared at her reflection in the mirror. The braid was turning out much better this time. All she had to do was tie it and she'd be set.

Jessica pounded on the door again. "Hurry up!" she ordered.

"If you'd quit bugging me, I'd get done a lot faster," Elizabeth replied.

"If you'd quit hogging the bathroom, we'd *all* get done a lot faster." Jessica groaned.

The braids were done. Now the question was, should she wear the rest of her hair in front of her shoulders or behind them?

"If you don't come out of there right now, I'm coming in!" Jessica yelled.

Elizabeth rolled her eyes. "Fine," she said, opening the door. "You can come in."

"It's about time," Jessica sniffed. She blinked when she saw Elizabeth's braids. "Why are you wearing your hair like that?"

Elizabeth touched her braids self-consciously. "W-W-What do you mean?" she sputtered. "I always wear my hair back."

"Not in French braids, you don't." Jessica wrinkled her nose like she smelled something awful. "You're trying to impress that guy. That's what you're doing."

"So?" Elizabeth said, noting Jessica's brand-new jeans and blouse. "What about you? Those look like awfully nice clothes for a casual day on the ranch."

Jessica put on a fake smile. "It only seems that way to you because I'm a much better dresser than you are." She put her hands on her hips. "You'd better get your fashion sense in gear if you think you can compete with me. I'm going riding today too."

"Oh, please," Elizabeth said, brushing past her sister. "You, ride? Since when are you interested in horses?"

"Since when do you hog the bathroom?" Jessica retorted.

Elizabeth scowled. "Well, I met the mystery guy in the barn. That means he's into riding, which is something you're not. So we obviously have something in common."

"He's not going to care once he sees how well dressed I am." Jessica pushed up her fancy cowboy hat with her right thumb and gave her sister a smug look.

"We'll see about that, Jessica," Elizabeth said as she stormed out of the cabin. *What makes her think she can act this way?* she wondered. *Is she actually going to go horseback riding just to impress some guy? What's gotten into her?*

Elizabeth stopped in her tracks. *Probably the same thing that had me working on my hair for a half hour this morning,* she realized with alarm.

When Elizabeth got to the barn, the boy was already there, standing off in a corner by himself. He was wearing black jeans, a black cowboy hat, and a green shirt that matched his eyes perfectly.

"That's him, all right!"

Elizabeth jumped. Jessica had snuck up behind her and whispered in her ear.

"Sure is," Elizabeth agreed as her heart sank a little. She was hoping Jessica's "boyfriend" would turn out to be somebody other than the boy she'd seen in the barn yesterday. But no such luck. *Like I can compete with Jessica for a guy*, she thought. *Yeah, right.*

Jessica sauntered over to him like she owned the whole world, leaving Elizabeth behind. Elizabeth's face reddened with anger as she heard Jessica say, "So, we meet again," loudly enough for her to hear.

The boy looked up at her sister. "Well, hello," he said, grinning.

"Nice shirt," Jessica complimented him.

Elizabeth groaned. *I can't stand this*, she thought. *Why am I standing here watching my sister flirt with the guy I like?*

"Thanks," he replied.

"Is it new? I know some people wouldn't bring brand-new clothes to a dude ranch," Jessica said, glancing over her shoulder toward Elizabeth. "But I believe in always looking my best. I can see that you do too."

Elizabeth got so furious, she thought she'd explode. "I've had enough of this," she muttered. "I'm going to stop this if it's the last thing I do." Elizabeth's face burned with anger as she stormed over toward her sister and the dark-haired mystery boy.

The boy scratched his ear. "Well, it's not exactly brand-new," he admitted. Then he noticed Elizabeth.

His jaw dropped. He glanced from one twin to the other. "Wow! There are two of you," he said in a shocked voice.

It was a lot like what Mrs. Hogan had said. It had bugged Elizabeth then, but for some reason it didn't sound as bad coming from him.

He slapped his hand to his head. "I'm sorry," he said, shaking his head. "I know twins hate it when you say things like that—"

"Oh, that's OK," Jessica said, laughing. "We don't mind."

"Yeah, we're used to it," Elizabeth added.

Jessica frowned at her. "Well, in case you're wondering, I'm Jessica," she said, flipping her hair over her shoulder. "We met outside your cabin yesterday." She said it as though she was the only girl he could have seen all day.

Jessica's going to make a fool out of you if you don't speak up, Elizabeth told herself. She cleared her throat. "And I—I—I'm Elizabeth," she said, holding out her hand. "We met down here. In the barn."

The boy smiled as he shook her hand.

He's touching my hand, Elizabeth thought as her heart pounded hard enough to escape from her chest. *He's really touching my hand.* She couldn't resist sneaking a victorious glance at Jessica.

Jessica rolled her eyes as she stood tapping her foot. "Well, now that we have that all sorted out—" she began.

A tall man with graying hair interrupted. "Nick?" The man turned to Jessica. "Excuse me, miss," he said politely. Then he turned back to the boy. "Nick, they're assigning horses. They want you to come and tell them how much riding you've done."

"OK, Dad," the boy replied. He turned to Jessica and Elizabeth. "See you around," he said, tipping his hat. Then he followed the man out of the barn.

Elizabeth sighed. She'd hardly had a chance to say more than two words to the guy. But at least she found out his name: Nick. That was progress.

Jessica scowled at Elizabeth. "What did you hold out your hand like that for? Did you think he was going to kiss it or something?" she asked.

"No!" Elizabeth exclaimed. "It's polite to shake hands with someone when you meet them. But then again, you wouldn't know about manners."

Jessica shrugged. "You're so old-fashioned," she argued.

"Well, maybe Nick is an old-fashioned kind of guy," Elizabeth retorted.

"Yeah, right." Jessica snorted. "Well, I'm not going to stand here and argue with you."

"Good!" Elizabeth replied. "All you're doing is wasting my time."

"In fact, I don't even want to talk to you until after Nick chooses me over you," Jessica said, folding her arms across her chest. "Arguing with you just takes too much out of me."

Elizabeth burst out laughing. "Yeah, well, arguing with you takes a lot out of me too," she said. "But remember, once we're out riding, it's possible that Nick will choose me instead."

"Not in this lifetime," Jessica said as she headed out to join the riding group.

"You'd better watch it, Jess." Elizabeth grinned as she followed her twin sister out of the barn. "You'll be feeling a lot more humble once we get on those horses."

Mr. Hogan was addressing the crowd of Triple Z Ranch guests that had assembled outside the barn. "We've got a pretty big group this week," Mr. Hogan commented. "I think we'll break into two groups for the trail rides. I can take one group and Andy Hillestad here can take the other."

"Sure thing." Mr. Hillestad tipped his hat.

Elizabeth realized that she and Jessica were standing in the middle of the group. Nick was way over on one side, on the right. It was possible Nick would end up in one group and she in another. Even worse, it was possible that Mr. Hogan would divide the group right between her and Jessica and she'd end up in a group by herself while Jessica ended up in a group with Nick.

If that happened, Elizabeth might as well give up on Nick altogether. If Jessica and Nick got to spend the whole day together, alone, Jessica would definitely get her way. Elizabeth's heart ached just thinking about it.

She took two steps closer to Jessica. *There. That should do it*, she thought. *Mr. Hogan can't split the group right between me and Jessica anymore.*

"Hey!" Jessica whispered, shoving Elizabeth. "Move over! You're invading my personal space."

Invading her space! Elizabeth thought as she recovered her footing. She looked around and discovered Jessica had pushed her over to the left, toward the barn. Elizabeth was even farther away from Nick now.

Elizabeth could hardly believe she was fighting with Jessica over a guy. But there was something about him that Elizabeth really liked. And she wanted to give him a chance to like her back without Jessica worming her way in and ruining everything.

So while Mr. Hogan continued talking about the trails they'd be riding, Elizabeth inched her way back to the right, toward Nick.

"Elizabeth!" Jessica hissed, her eyes blazing. "Get back on that side!"

"I belong on this side," Elizabeth said through her teeth. "At least I did before you pushed me out."

"Well, if you don't get back over there, I'll push you again," Jessica said, bumping her shoulder into Elizabeth yet again.

"Jessica! Stop it!" *Push.*

"No, you stop it!" *Push push.*

"Cut it out!" *Shove.*

"*You* cut it out, Elizabeth!" *Shove shove shove.*

The twins had worked their way around the corner of the barn, out of sight from the group. They locked arms and were pushing against each other. All of a sudden Elizabeth's arms gave out. She felt herself falling backward. Jessica fell forward.

The two landed with a splash. Right in a puddle of mud.

"I can't believe you," Jessica said angrily as she stomped up the hill to the cabins, wiping her dirty hands on her brand-new jeans.

"You pushed me first!" Elizabeth glared at Jessica as she fell into step with her.

"As far as I'm concerned, that's beside the point." Jessica examined Lila's cowboy hat for mud spots and grimaced. "Look at what you've done. We're both covered in mud. And now neither of us will get to go riding with Nick."

"If we hurry up, maybe we can get back down in time," Elizabeth replied. "All I have to do is throw on some clean clothes. You, however, have your whole beauty ritual to start over."

Jessica frowned. *When did Elizabeth get to be such a dirty fighter?* she wondered. "I had no idea you were so vicious, Elizabeth. I mean, he's just a guy. I thought you said you'd take a horse over a guy any day."

"I told you yesterday there was something different about him." Elizabeth burst through the door to their cabin. "I told you I really liked this guy. And now you want to have him all to yourself."

"Yeah, you like him so much that you'd pull your only sister into a puddle of mud just so *you* can have him to *your*self!" Jessica yelled as she stormed after her sister to their bedroom.

Elizabeth yanked open her bureau drawer. "I didn't pull you into that puddle. You pushed us both into it," she said, pointing at Jessica.

Jessica peeled off her muddy jeans. "Well, none of this would've happened if you stuck to your precious horses. Why are you so interested in Nick anyway? What about Todd Wilkins? Don't you care about him anymore?"

Elizabeth's jaw dropped, and Jessica felt triumphant. Todd was Elizabeth's sort-of boyfriend back at Sweet Valley Middle School, and Jessica knew that comment would get her where it really hurt.

"Todd and I are good friends, but we're not married or anything." Elizabeth went into the bathroom and came out with a wet washcloth, which she ran back and forth along her muddy arm. "Besides, what do you care about Todd? I didn't think you even liked him all that much."

"I don't know whatever gave you that idea," Jessica said innocently. "I just think it's really mean of you not to take his feelings into consideration here. I mean, you've only been apart for what? Two days? And you're already going after another guy."

Elizabeth folded her arms across her chest. "Well, if you're so concerned about other people's feelings, what about Aaron Dallas's?" she asked smugly.

"Oh, please." Jessica rolled her eyes, grabbed another pair of almost-new jeans, and put her legs into them. "Aaron and I see other people. He wouldn't mind."

"Sure, he wouldn't," Elizabeth said, buttoning up her clean new shirt.

Jessica noticed Elizabeth had a smudge of mud on her cheek. She decided not to tell her about it. "Well, Nick and I will see you on the trail," she said sweetly, scampering off her bed and out toward the door.

Elizabeth tucked her shirt into her jeans. "I'm right behind you," she said just before Jessica closed the door. "Try not to scare the horses *too* much, OK?"

Horses! Jessica realized. Oh, no, she'd have to get on the stupid things after all!

*   *   *

Jessica grinned when Elizabeth caught up to her. "Oh, look!" Jessica pointed toward the stables. "Nick waited for me."

"Maybe he's waiting for me," Elizabeth responded.

Mr. Hogan and Mr. Hillestad were helping people onto the horses. But Nick was lingering at the back of the crowd, waving at the twins.

"Hello, Elizabeth," he called as the twins approached.

"I don't hear him saying, 'Hi, Jessica,'" Elizabeth said, gloating.

Jessica felt her back stiffen. She glared at her sister, then hurried toward the boy. "Hi, Nick," she said cheerfully. "It was so nice of you to wait for me."

Nick smiled at Jessica, but when Elizabeth approached, he held out his hand. "Hello again, Elizabeth," he said, smiling even wider at her. "I'm Nick Handel."

"Nice to see you again, Nick," Elizabeth replied, shooting a triumphant look at her sister.

Jessica felt her blood boiling. She'd never felt so angry in her entire life. *I might as well go back to the cabin*, she thought wearily. *In fact, we might as well all head back to Sweet Valley. Nick chose my boring sister over me!*

"There's somebody here I'd like you both to meet," Nick said. He stepped aside to reveal another guy in a blue shirt with his back turned to them. Nick tapped him on the shoulder.

Not only was the new guy the same height as Nick, but he had the same dark wavy hair that Nick had.

When he turned around, Jessica gasped. So did Elizabeth.

Aside from the fact the new guy was wearing a blue shirt and Nick was wearing a green one, the two boys looked exactly alike.

Five

"I'm Chris Handel," the other boy said, offering his hand to Jessica. "We met outside our cabins yesterday."

"And I saw you down here in the barn," Nick told Elizabeth.

"Oh!" Elizabeth said, glancing from one identical brother to the other.

"Oh!" Jessica echoed.

Elizabeth looked at Jessica. The two stared at each other in stunned silence for a bit. Then they burst out laughing.

"What?" Nick asked, looking confused. "What's so funny?"

Elizabeth forced herself to calm down.

Jessica cleared her throat. "Uh, nothing," she responded, winking at Elizabeth.

"While you were gone, we made sure you were both assigned to our trail group," Nick informed them.

"Yeah, why don't you get your horses and meet us at the start of the trail," Chris added.

"OK," Jessica said eagerly.

"We'll see you in a few minutes," Elizabeth added.

As soon as the boys were gone the twins turned to each other again.

"Can you believe it?" Jessica squealed.

"Twins!" Elizabeth squealed right back.

"This couldn't have turned out more perfect," Jessica said, sighing.

"No, it couldn't have," Elizabeth agreed, feeling relaxed and happy for the first time that day. What had started out as a nice family vacation had just gotten ten times better. Aside from the fact she and Jessica had just wasted part of it fighting.

As they walked along the paddock fence Elizabeth grabbed her sister's arm. "Hey, Jess," she said. "Let's never fight over a boy again, OK?"

Jessica nodded. "Agreed," she said, holding out her hand.

The twins shook hands, then headed for the barn.

"You're the brother of those twin girls, aren't you?" Mr. Hogan asked.

"Yes," Steven said, sighing. *Is that how I'm going*

to be known all week? he wondered. *The brother of the twin girls?*

"Let's see," Mr. Hogan said, gazing at the clipboard in his hand. "Andy put you with Queenie, the black mare with the white star."

"Well, actually I was hoping I could ride Rocket," Steven said casually.

"Rocket?" Mr. Hogan stared at Steven with disbelief.

"Yeah." Steven nodded eagerly. "She's the one who ran in the California Derby years ago, right?"

Mr. Hogan scratched his head. "Well, yeah, but—"

"Then she's the horse I want!" Steven said emphatically.

"Well, we don't usually assign Rocket—"

"I can handle her, Mr. Hogan, really I can!" Steven begged. "When I saw her out back yesterday, I just fell in love with her. Please let me take her. Please!"

Mr. Hogan looked doubtful. "Well, if you insist," he said, shrugging.

"I do," Steven said.

As Mr. Hogan headed back to the barn Steven rubbed his hands together in excitement. He had managed to snag the fastest horse at the ranch. That cowboy hat they were giving away on the last day was as good as his!

"Here you go, miss." Mr. Hillestad handed

Jessica the reins of a handsome bay quarter horse. "This is Goody Two-shoes."

"Goody Two-shoes, huh?" Jessica said uncertainly as she reached up to pet the horse just above its nose. She'd seen Elizabeth do that to Nick's horse a few minutes earlier, and his horse seemed to like it. But Goody Two-shoes just raised her head and snorted.

Jessica quickly pulled her hand away. "Aaah! Don't bite me!" she yelled.

"She won't hurt you," Mr. Hillestad assured her.

"Oh, I know that," Jessica said, forcing a smile. After all, she didn't want Chris and Nick to think she was afraid of horses.

She wasn't afraid, exactly. It was just that she had an understanding with most horses on the planet: they wouldn't bother her as long as she didn't go near them.

"Just put your left foot up in this stirrup here and swing your right leg up and over," Mr. Hillestad instructed.

Out of the corner of her eye Jessica saw Chris perched on top of a tan-colored horse over by the barn. *If anything's going to get me on a horse*, she thought, *that's it, right there.*

Jessica flipped her hair over her shoulder. "OK," she said, turning back to Mr. Hillestad. *I have to make this look like I know what I'm doing*, she told herself. *Well, here goes nothing.* She gritted her teeth and put her left foot up in the stirrup just as Mr.

Hillestad instructed. She put her hand on the saddle horn and pulled. She felt like she was going to pull the saddle right off the horse, but somehow she managed to swing her leg up and over. Her behind landed in the saddle with a plop.

Whew! She breathed a sigh of relief and flipped her hair over her shoulder again.

But suddenly the horse whinnied and stamped the ground with her front hooves. Jessica instinctively grabbed the horse's mane. It felt rough in her hands.

"Get me off this thing!" Jessica screamed as the horse reared up.

"Hang on, Jess!" Elizabeth cried, running toward her.

"Easy, girl," Mr. Hillestad said soothingly as he grabbed the horse's reins.

"This horse is totally out of control," Jessica complained as Goody Two-shoes snorted again, then planted her feet on the ground. "She doesn't belong on a dude ranch. She belongs in a glue factory!"

"Jessica!" Elizabeth cried, glaring up at her. "How could you say such a thing!" She stroked the horse's nose exactly the same way Jessica had before she got on. But this time Goody Two-shoes nickered softly and rested her head on Elizabeth's shoulder.

Jessica rolled her eyes. *Stupid horse!* she thought. *I don't know why we had to ruin a perfect vacation by going horseback riding anyway.*

"Maybe I could ride this horse," Elizabeth said. "You can try my horse, Jess."

"Or we've got a milder-mannered horse you could try," Mr. Hillestad offered.

"No, thanks," Jessica said, swinging her leg back over the horse and jumping down. "I've had enough horseback riding for one day. I think I'll head back to the lodge and see what there is to do back there."

"You're going to *what?*" Chris asked, sounding disappointed.

Jessica turned. She hadn't heard him or his horse approach.

"Uh, I meant after the trail ride," she said quickly. "After the trail ride I'm going to see what else there is to do around here." She turned back to Mr. Hillestad. "I'd love to try that other horse you've got," she said, smiling sweetly.

"He's right over there," Mr. Hillestad said, pointing at a gray-spotted horse at the far end of the pasture. "His name's Sleepy."

"He looks perfect," Jessica told Mr. Hillestad. She was actually looking at Chris, and not the horse, when she said it. Her heart was pounding wildly, but she wasn't sure if it was because Chris was so gorgeous or because she was so terrified of getting on another horse. *Who cares*, she said to herself. *If it means spending time alone with that guy, it'll all be worth it!*

* * *

Something was wrong. *This horse just isn't behaving the way a racehorse should,* Steven thought.

Steven pressed his heels into the horse's flanks a little harder. Rocket groaned and snorted. She lurched forward and went a little faster for about thirty seconds. Then she slowed again.

I could crawl *faster than this,* Steven thought with annoyance as the horse named Queenie edged up behind him.

The guy who was riding Queenie was the father of those boys his sisters were mooning over. He nodded at Steven, who had to steer Rocket over to the side to let him pass.

Steven turned around in his saddle. "Hey," he called to Mr. Hillestad. "I thought this was a racehorse."

Mr. Hillestad laughed. "That was many years ago, son. She's still got a little kick left, but she doesn't put out the effort much anymore. I tried to tell you, but you were so insistent."

"We'll leave the light on for you when we get back, Steven," Mr. Wakefield teased as he steered his palomino around Rocket.

"Ned!" Mrs. Wakefield admonished as she followed her husband. "Don't give Steven a hard time." She was riding a pretty gray horse with dark spots on his rump.

"I'll try and slip back to the end of the line from

time to time to make sure you're doing OK," Mr. Hillestad promised. "But for the most part I'll be in the lead." He clucked his tongue and his palomino took off at a gentle clip.

Steven sighed. Andy had said Rocket had some kick left. Maybe once he got used to her, Steven could make her use it. For now, though, he found himself at the back of the ride. All alone.

"Of course, the Unicorn Club takes a lot of my time," Jessica told Chris as they rode side by side along the grassy trail. She thought he had a right to know she was associated with the most exclusive club at school. Besides, talking kept her mind off the fact that she was actually sitting on the back of a moving horse.

Chris looked at her with interest. "So what does the Unicorn Club do?"

"Do?" Jessica said, as though she'd never heard the word before.

"Yeah. What's its purpose?"

Well, one of the main purposes was to talk about boys, but Jessica knew she couldn't very well tell Chris that. "We ensure the social well-being of every Sweet Valley Middle School student," she said finally.

She'd heard that line somewhere before. It was in the Declaration of Independence or one of those old documents. If it was good enough for the whole country, it was good enough for the Unicorn Club.

"Your club sounds like a very noble organization," Chris said, obviously impressed.

Jessica grinned. "Oh, it is," she agreed, her blue-green eyes sparkling. "I'm also on the Boosters, which is a cheering and baton squad. We cheer at all the important games."

"Really?" Chris raised one eyebrow.

Jessica's heart pounded when he did that. *This guy is so incredibly cute!* she thought. *I have to get a picture of him to show Lila Fowler. She's going to be so jealous!*

"Gee, we don't even have a cheering squad at our middle school," Chris remarked. "Our school is so small that everybody is already on the team. There isn't anybody left to stand on the sidelines and cheer."

Jessica laughed as she pulled on the reins and steered Sleepy around a corner. *I may be getting the hang of this,* she thought. Then the horse snorted and bucked slightly, and Jessica swallowed her confidence. "So, where are you from anyway?" she asked nervously.

"I'm from Merrill Falls, Nevada," Chris replied. He squinched up his nose. "You've never heard of it, have you?"

Jessica shook her head. "Can't say that I have."

"Where are you from?" Chris asked.

Jessica loved how he looked right at her when

he asked her a question. He was so much more mature than all the boys back home. She ignored Sleepy's snorting and looked right back into his eyes. "I'm from Sweet Valley, California," she said. "It's only about an hour from here."

"Near L.A.?" Chris raised an eyebrow again.

"Pretty near."

"We have a bus that goes from Merrill Falls to L.A. every other day," Chris said.

Jessica's heart soared. He was already talking about visiting her after this week was over!

"I actually like school," Elizabeth admitted sheepishly to Nick. "Do you think that's weird?"

"No," Nick replied. He and Elizabeth were riding a few yards ahead of Chris and Jessica.

"I'd probably like school better if I was any good at it," Nick went on. "Movies are more my thing."

"Movies?" Elizabeth asked curiously. "Do you mean filming them or acting in them?"

Nick shrugged. "Both. Maybe even writing or directing."

"Writing?" Elizabeth's heart skipped a beat. Nick was into writing too!

"Sure," Nick replied. His green eyes sparkled as he grew more excited. "There's a lot more that goes into moviemaking than most people know about. There's the writing, the casting, the directing, the filming, the editing—and I want to have a chance to try it all! At least until I figure out what I'm good at."

"I bet you'd be good at any of it," Elizabeth said with devotion.

"Yeah?" Nick turned to her. "How do you know? You hardly know me."

"I can see the way your whole face lights up when you talk about it," she responded.

"I guess you could say it's my passion," Nick said, shrugging. "I just wish I had a chance to really learn about filmmaking. But a hick town like Merrill Falls, Nevada, doesn't offer much. You're so lucky to live so close to L.A.!"

Elizabeth stroked her horse's neck. Goody Two-shoes nickered softly in response.

"Well," she said. "I like Sweet Valley OK. But L.A.'s a little big for my tastes. You can't go horse-back riding there. At least not right in Hollywood."

Nick glanced toward the snowcapped mountains in the distance. "Yeah, well, horseback riding isn't everything," he said softly.

"Did you girls have a good time?" Mrs. Wakefield asked as the two sets of twins rode to a stop by the barn.

"Yeah, it was great," Elizabeth replied with a grin. She swung her leg over the back of her horse and jumped to the ground.

"The horseback riding wasn't bad either," Jessica said, grinning. "Except for my sore muscles.

Ow!" Jessica massaged the backs of her legs.

Elizabeth laughed. "If you're sore now, wait till you get down from the horse," she warned her twin.

"Great." Jessica groaned. "*If* I can get down from this thing."

Elizabeth came over to pet Sleepy. "So, it sounds like you and Chris hit it off," she said casually.

"Shhh!" Jessica hissed. She motioned for Elizabeth to look behind her. Chris and Nick were walking toward them with their parents.

Chris walked right over to Jessica. "Can I help you down?" he asked politely as he reached for her hand.

Jessica smiled. "Sure," she responded. She lifted her leg over the horse, grabbed Chris's hand, and jumped down.

"You must be Mrs. Wakefield." Chris and Nick's mom approached Elizabeth and Jessica's mom. "I'm Leah Handel and this is my husband, Chad. We wanted to introduce ourselves since our children seem to have made friends."

Mr. and Mrs. Handel were both tall, with dark hair and green eyes, just like their sons. Mrs. Handel's hair was tied back in a ponytail.

"I'm glad you did," Mrs. Wakefield replied. "I'm Alice Wakefield and that's my husband, Ned, over there with our son, Steven." She pointed to the far end of the barn, where Mr. Wakefield and Steven were deep in conversation with one of the ranch hands.

Chris and Nick exchanged looks. "Go on," Nick said, nudging his brother.

Chris cleared his throat and took a step closer to Mrs. Wakefield. "Uh, we were wondering whether you'd give us permission to have dinner with Jessica and Elizabeth tonight." He cleared his throat again, then added one more word. "Alone."

Jessica looked at Elizabeth, who was biting her lip. She looked as excited as Jessica felt.

"Well," Mrs. Wakefield said, smiling. "It's OK with me if you girls want to."

"Yes, we do!" Jessica burst out. Then she got control of herself. "Um, I mean, that would be fine. Right, Elizabeth?" Jessica elbowed her.

Elizabeth nodded. "It would be great."

"Good," Chris said.

"How about we meet in the dining hall at six-thirty," Nick suggested.

"OK," Elizabeth and Jessica replied in unison. They looked at each other. Riding was one thing. But dinner together? That was a date!

"Perhaps we could have dinner too," Mrs. Wakefield suggested to Mr. and Mrs. Handel.

"That would be nice." Mrs. Handel smiled in response.

"Same time?" Mrs. Wakefield asked. "Six-thirty?"

"Mo-om!" Jessica whispered. *That'd be just perfect*, she thought gloomily. *Here we are going on a real double date and* all *our parents will be there.*

"Let's make it seven-thirty," Mrs. Handel said.

"And you four will have our word that we'll stay on the *other* side of the dining hall," Mrs. Wakefield said, and all the adults laughed.

"We'll be there," Mr. Handel replied.

Once the Handels were gone, Elizabeth turned to Jessica. "Isn't that sweet? They asked our parents' permission. Just like in the olden days when the boy would ask the girl's parents for permission to marry her," she said, sighing.

Jessica rolled her eyes. "Personally, I thought that was a little embarrassing," she responded.

"Well, it was *your* date, Chris, who did it," Elizabeth pointed out.

"Oh." Jessica blinked. "In that case, you're right. It is sweet."

Six

"I can see it now," Jessica said, holding her hands in front of her as though she were looking through a window. "We're going to have a double wedding. Me and Chris. You and Nick. Five hundred of our closest friends. It's going to be great."

The girls were getting ready for dinner. Elizabeth was buttoning her white blouse. Her blue-flowered skirt was lying on her bed. But Jessica's clothes were still spread out over her bed, Elizabeth's bed, and the floor.

Elizabeth tried to ignore the mess and concentrate on the boys. "It would be neat if we had a double wedding, wouldn't it?" she said, starry-eyed. "Especially if we were getting married to twins."

"We will!" Jessica insisted. "I can feel it."

Jessica often told people she was psychic, and usually Elizabeth didn't put a lot of stock in it. But this time, when Jessica insisted that they'd have a double wedding, it gave Elizabeth goose bumps.

"But first I need to figure out what to wear tonight." Jessica sighed as she stared at the mound of clothes on her bed. "What do you think, Lizzie? This one?" She held up a striped sleeveless dress with a matching belt.

"That's nice." Elizabeth nodded.

Jessica wrinkled her nose. "Yeah, but I think it's too dressy for this place." She tossed the dress back onto her bed and picked up a denim skirt and a ruffled blouse. "What about this?"

"That's nice too," Elizabeth said. "And it looks really western."

"Yeah, but it's more you than me," Jessica complained, throwing both the skirt and blouse down. "It's important that our true identities show through. We don't want the boys to wonder who's who." She threw on a long flowered sundress with a nipped-in waist. "How about this one?"

"That's perfect, Jess," Elizabeth replied absently. She was deep in thought. *Nick and Chris may be able to figure out who's who from* our *clothes*, Elizabeth realized. *But what if they're dressed alike and we can't tell* them *apart?*

Jessica zipped up the dress and put on a pair of sandals. She gave her hair one last brush and turned to Elizabeth. "Are we ready, or are we ready?"

"We're ready, already," Elizabeth replied. "Let's go."

The twins headed over to the main lodge. Elizabeth was still concerned about telling the boys apart. "Hey, Jess?" Elizabeth asked worriedly. "What if they're dressed alike? What will we do?"

For a second Jessica looked worried. Then she shook her head. "Don't worry about that. If anybody can tell twins apart, it's twins!"

Elizabeth sighed. "You're right," she replied. But part of her was still unsure. *I hope she really is right*, Elizabeth thought, *or else this whole date could be a disaster!*

When the twins got to the dining hall, they couldn't believe their eyes. The Handel twins were waiting for them, and they couldn't tell which was which. The boys were both wearing nice white shirts, khakis, and sneakers. The only difference was that one of the twins was wearing Nike sneakers and the other was wearing Reebok sneakers.

"Hi, Jessica." The twin in Nike sneakers stepped forward.

"Chris?" Jessica asked, unsure.

"Uh-huh," Chris replied. "Glad to see you again."

"Me too," Jessica said, relieved.

"Hi, Nick," Elizabeth said to the boy in Reebok sneakers.

"How's it going, Elizabeth?" Nick asked.

A waiter stepped toward them. "Are you four looking for a table?" he asked. He had an amused smile on his face.

"Gee, how do you think he figured that out?" Jessica whispered to Elizabeth. Elizabeth giggled.

"Yes, thanks," Chris replied, and the waiter pointed at an empty table near the huge picture window.

Jessica's face reddened as they all walked to the empty table. Diners at every table were turning to stare at them and whisper to one another. *These people are acting like they've never seen twins before,* she thought angrily. *Can't they mind their own business?*

When the twins got to their table and sat down, a lady at the next table put her hand to her chest and smiled at her husband. "Oh, look!" she exclaimed, not making any effort to keep her voice quiet. "It's twin girls and twin boys. Did you ever see such a thing?"

"No, dear," he said, winking at the twins. "How do you suppose they manage to keep each other straight?"

Jessica rolled her eyes. "Look, you guys," she whispered as she leaned close to her friends. "It's a really obnoxious lady and her really obnoxious husband. How do you suppose they keep each other straight?"

Everyone laughed. But deep down Jessica didn't think it was very funny. She hated it when people thought she and Elizabeth were cute just because they were twins. And now that they were with another set of twins, people thought they were even cuter.

But Jessica didn't think this was cute at all. This was serious. This was love.

"So, do people mix you two up as much as they mix us up?" Nick asked.

"Yes," Elizabeth said, buttering one of the rolls that were in the basket on the table.

"All the time," Jessica chimed in.

"It just goes with the territory of being a twin," Chris said, reaching for a roll.

Nick turned to his brother. "Yeah, but if people would just take a second to think about it, they'd see how easy it is to tell us apart."

Chris nodded. "For instance, I'm right-handed and Nick is left-handed," he said, waving his fork at his brother.

"Yeah, and I wear Reebok sneakers and Chris wears Nike sneakers," Nick said.

"I wear a watch and Jessica doesn't," Elizabeth put in.

"And I have fashion sense and Elizabeth doesn't," Jessica sang out.

Elizabeth frowned.

"Well, it's true," Jessica said, shrugging.

"The point is, we're each unique. Just because we're twins doesn't mean we're two halves of a whole," Chris said, looking serious. "It gets really annoying to be constantly confused and mistaken."

"Well, I have to admit, sometimes that comes in handy," Jessica said with a glimmer in her eye.

The boys eyed her curiously.

"Haven't you guys ever, you know, switched identities?" Jessica asked mischievously.

The boys glanced at each other. Then they both burst out laughing.

"What?" Elizabeth asked, smiling. "Tell us!"

"Well, there was one time fairly recently when we switched places and even our parents couldn't tell us apart!" Nick exclaimed.

"Yeah," Chris said, wiping his hand across his mouth. "Mom and Dad had this idea that each of them should spend some quality time alone with each of us. So Mom made plans for her and me to go mountain climbing—"

"And Dad made plans for him and me to go fishing," Nick interrupted.

"Don't tell me," Jessica said, banging her hand on the table. "You guys switched places."

The boys looked at each other and nodded.

"That's why we're all here together," Chris admitted sheepishly. "Mom said there's no point in taking separate vacations if she can't even tell which twin she's actually with."

Elizabeth laughed. "You mean they never even figured it out?"

Nick shook his head. "Not until about a week later, when Chris made some dumb comment about something he and Dad did on their fishing trip." Nick nudged Chris with his elbow.

"Well, I have to say Elizabeth and I have pulled off some pretty good twin switches ourselves," Jessica said, squeezing her twin's shoulders.

"That's right," Elizabeth agreed. "We've fooled our teachers and our friends."

"Face it," Chris said. "If you put your mind to it, you can fool just about anybody."

"Well, don't try fooling us," Jessica said, laughing. "It takes a twin to know a twin. And we're pretty tough to fool."

"That's right," Nick agreed with a wink. "I don't think twins are as easily fooled as everyone else."

Jessica watched Chris as he sliced his square of lime Jell-O in half. Then in quarters. Then in eighths. Then in sixteenths. It was the most bizarre thing she'd ever seen.

He grinned at her as he speared one of the tiny squares with his fork, then popped it into his mouth.

Jessica forced herself to smile back. *But really!* she thought indignantly. *What kind of person cuts up his Jell-O into sixteen bite-size pieces?*

She stole a sideways glance at Nick. "Some people

don't like Jim Carrey, but I think he's a master," Nick was saying.

Elizabeth's chin was resting in her hands. She was leaning across the table, her eyes focused on Nick. She looked totally thrilled being with him. Jessica didn't blame her. Nick was cute and funny, and he knew a lot about movies.

"Aren't you going to eat your Jell-O?" Chris asked.

"Huh?" Jessica said, forcing her attention back to Chris.

"Your Jell-O," he said, pointing to Jessica's red Jell-O square. "If you don't want it, I'll take it."

"Uh, be my guest," she said, sliding her plate over to him. Then she watched as he proceeded to do the exact same thing to her square of Jell-O that he'd done to his own. Her eyes just about popped out of their sockets as she watched him line up the little squares: red, green, red, green.

Suddenly Elizabeth giggled.

Jessica turned to see what was so funny.

"Ace Ventura!" Nick said in a perfect Jim Carrey voice. "Pet detective!"

Jessica laughed. *Nick is funny*, she thought. *Is he funnier than Chris?*

She turned back to Chris, who was now building a pyramid out of his little Jell-O squares. *That's not very cool*, she thought disdainfully.

Jessica felt her heart begin to pound. *What if I'm with the wrong twin?* she thought in a panic. *I* definitely *belong with the cooler twin. What if Nick is actually cooler than Chris? This could be a catastrophe! I could find myself walking down the aisle with the wrong twin. Then what?*

I'd better fix things before they go any further, Jessica told herself.

But what about Elizabeth?

"Ace Ventura! Pet detective!" Nick said for about the thousandth time.

Elizabeth smiled politely and tried to look interested, but Jim Carrey was just not one of her top ten favorite actors. In fact, he wasn't even in the top one hundred. To be perfectly honest, Elizabeth thought he was kind of stupid.

Is Nick stupid too? she wondered.

Elizabeth glanced over at Jessica, who was gazing deeply into Chris's eyes. She couldn't blame her sister. Chris was so soulful, so sweet.

But Nick? Nick was so . . . weird. Elizabeth wasn't sure just how many more Jim Carrey imitations she could take.

"S-S-S-S-S-Smokin'!" Nick yelled, laughing as though he thought he was the funniest person on the planet. "S-S-S-S-S-Smokin'!"

What if I'm with the wrong twin? Elizabeth thought suddenly. *What if Chris is the one I'm destined to be with? What would Jessica say if I told her I actually liked Chris better than Nick? Jessica wouldn't be very happy.*

What am I going to do? Elizabeth rested her chin in her hands and sighed. *I can't keep going on dates with Nick when I really like Chris.*

But what about Jessica?

"Did you, uh, have a good time tonight?" Elizabeth asked Jessica as they were getting ready for bed.

"Yeah," Jessica said, smiling brightly. "Did you?"

"Sure," Elizabeth replied. She watched as Jessica brushed her long hair. "Did it seem like you and Chris have a lot in common?" she asked carefully.

"Oh, yeah." Jessica nodded. "We have loads of stuff in common."

"Good," Elizabeth said, forcing a smile. *If only she felt the same way I did*, she thought morosely. *Then everything would be perfect.*

She got into bed and pulled the covers up to her chin. She couldn't tell Jessica about how much she liked Chris. Not if Jessica and Chris were getting along so well.

"Good night, Lizzie," Jessica said, turning out the light.

"Good night, Jess," Elizabeth replied. She rolled over so she was facing the wall instead of her sister. *Maybe things will look better in the morning,* she told herself as she drifted off to sleep.

"Come along, Jessica. We mustn't be late for the

opera," a grown-up Chris said. He was dressed in a black tuxedo with tails.

Jessica was wearing a long, plain black skirt with a white blouse that buttoned all the way up to her chin. Her shoes were shapeless and mushy looking.

"What is this?" Nick asked, bending down and picking up one of Jessica's socks. "Remember, darling. There's a place for every thing and a thing for every place." He took the sock over to the hamper and dropped it in.

"I'm sorry," Jessica heard herself say. "I'll try to remember next time."

Just then two kids bounded into the room. The boy looked exactly like Chris and the girl looked exactly like Jessica.

"Remember, Mother," the girl said. "I've got my knitting lesson tomorrow."

"Yes, and I've got my bird-calling class," the boy piped up.

Jessica stared at them. Knitting? Bird calling? Were these her kids?

"Don't worry, children," Chris said, ruffling them each on the head. "We don't expect the opera to last much later than eight o'clock. That means we'll be home and ready for bed by eight-thirty. Your mom won't have any trouble getting up for your five A.M. bird-calling class."

"Five A.M.!" Jessica gaped at Chris. "You mean, like, five A.M. in the morning?"

Chris frowned. "Of course," he replied. "You know

we get up early in this house, Jessica. If you wanted to lie around and be lazy, you should've married my brother!"

"Mom! Mom, I'm going over to Tommy's to go bungee jumping. Dad said I could!"

Elizabeth blinked. Where was she? Who was this little boy, and why was he calling her Mom? He looked just like Nick.

"Bungee jumping? You're only five!" Elizabeth said, shocked. "Where's your father?"

"Where he usually is, Mom. On the couch!" the boy chirped as he ran out the door before Elizabeth could stop him.

The couch? Elizabeth walked through the strange house. The walls were covered with pictures of Jim Carrey. Ugh. Was this where she lived?

"Nick?" she called weakly. "Nick, where are you?"

"Ha-haaaaaaa!" A loud, obnoxious laugh rang through the house. Elizabeth followed it to its source.

Nick was lying down on a couch, watching TV. Ace Ventura: Pet Detective was playing on the VCR. Nick picked up a remote and rewound the tape a little, then started laughing again. He rewound it, laughed, rewound it, laughed, and rewound it and laughed some more.

"You've gotta see this, honey," Nick said, looking away from the TV for a brief moment. "This is the best part."

"Not again, Nick. You've worn out five Ace Ventura

tapes already." Elizabeth stopped herself. How did she know that?

"I went out and bought another one today, dear. You know I can't make it through the day without watching at least one Jim Carrey movie." He looked back at the TV, then at Elizabeth. "I mean, why make movies when it's more fun watching them, right?" He looked back at the TV and started laughing hysterically.

Elizabeth buried her face in her hands.

"Aaaaaaaah! Aaaaaaaah! Oh, no, help! Aaaaaaaugh!"

Who was that? Elizabeth looked around. It wasn't her. Wait a minute . . . that sounds just like . . .

Jessica!

"Jessica! Jessica, are you OK?" Elizabeth called, waking herself up. The covers were twisted in her hands. Sweat poured down her face. *It was just a dream*, she told herself. *Everything's OK. Jessica wasn't really crying for help.* She breathed a sigh of relief and slowly eased her head back onto her pillow.

"Ooooohh, no, not five in the morning! Pleeeeease, help meeeee!"

Elizabeth jolted and turned to see that Jessica was thrashing around in her bed in the throes of a nightmare. She jumped over to her sister's bed and shook Jessica's shoulders. "Wake up, Jess!" she said. "Calm down. Everything's OK."

"Wha—?" Jessica woke with a start. "Lizzie, I just had the most horrible dream!"

"I know. Do you want to talk about it?"

Jessica looked uneasy. "No, I'd rather not. I—I don't think I'm ready to."

"I understand," Elizabeth said. *More than you know,* she thought. "Are you OK?"

"I think so. Let's just go back to sleep, all right?"

"All right," Elizabeth responded. She climbed back into bed and glanced over at Jessica. *Poor Jess,* she thought. *She's having awful nightmares while I'm plotting how to take Chris away.* A wave of guilt washed over her. But much as she hated to hurt her sister's feelings, Elizabeth knew that there was no way she could keep pretending that she liked Nick. That dream proved it to her; it would never work out. She needed to change things before it was too late.

Wait till tomorrow, she told herself, checking her watch by the moonlight. *There's no use losing sleep over it now.*

"Hey, Jess," Elizabeth whispered.

"What, Lizzie?" Jessica asked weakly.

"How did you know it was five in the morning?"

Seven

The next morning Jessica and her twin stood side by side in the bathroom, doing their hair. "Nick is really cool, isn't he?" Jessica asked.

Elizabeth glanced at Jessica in the mirror. "Sure," she replied as she fastened a barrette in her hair. "So's Chris."

"Yeah," Jessica said, shrugging. "He's kind of serious, though, don't you think? Not that serious is bad. Dad's serious. Doesn't Chris sort of remind you of Dad?"

Elizabeth blinked. "Uh, yeah," she said cheerfully. "I imagine that's why you like him so much. People always say a girl will marry a guy just like her father." With that, Elizabeth put down her brush and left the room.

Jessica sighed. Elizabeth hadn't taken her hint at all.

Go after her, a voice inside Jessica said. *Tell her you think she should go out with Chris and you should go out with Nick.* But somehow Jessica just couldn't bring herself to do that. She could see how much her sister liked Nick too. Her whole face just lit up whenever his name was mentioned. But she didn't react at all when Chris's name came up.

Jessica couldn't steal her sister's boyfriend right out from under her. But she couldn't go on dating Chris as though everything was fine either.

What was she going to do?

As Jessica was on her way to the stables she noticed Nick down by the paddock. She knew it was him because he was wearing Reebok sneakers and had a video camera. He seemed to be filming the mountains in the distance.

Jessica reached into her pocket, pulled out a watch, and put it on. She felt a little guilty about what she was going to do. But she had to get to know Nick a little. She had to make sure he really was the one for her before she went and broke the news to Elizabeth.

She took a deep breath and walked over to Nick. "Hi," she said shyly.

Nick put down his camera and turned to Jessica. He looked a little confused, so Jessica made a point of looking at her watch. "I see we've still got a while before the trail ride this morning."

"It is you, Elizabeth," Nick said, grinning with relief.

"You mean you couldn't tell?" Jessica said, batting her eyes flirtatiously.

"Well," Nick admitted, scratching his chin. "You *are* wearing your hair the way Jessica wore hers yesterday."

Oops! Almost got busted there, Jessica scolded herself. *Think fast!* She flipped her hair over her shoulder. "Which way do you like it best?"

"I like it both ways," Nick said quickly.

"Oh," Jessica said, trying not to sound disappointed. She was hoping Nick would notice there was something different about "Elizabeth" right now. Something he liked better.

They walked along the paddock a little farther. Suddenly Nick turned to Jessica. "I do have to say I like the outfit you're wearing today better than the one you were wearing yesterday."

"You do!" Jessica squealed, glancing down at her white shirt with the black ribbing and her black jeans.

"Yeah, it's very western," Nick commented. "You look like you really belong out on the open range."

Jessica could hardly contain her excitement. She was definitely the twin with the fashion sense. They had established that fact last night. Now if only Nick would remember that. If only he'd say, "You're not actually Elizabeth, are you? You're really Jessica." Then his face would light up and he'd say, "I'm so glad it's you, Jessica. You're the one I want to date." Or perhaps his face would cloud up with concern and he'd confide in her: "Elizabeth, I hate to tell you this. But Jessica is the girl I really want to be with." That would be perfect. Plus Elizabeth couldn't blame her if Nick made the move.

Well, if being Elizabeth is what it takes to get close to Nick, Jessica reasoned, *then I'll be Elizabeth—for now. But how can I keep Elizabeth from finding out?*

"Here you go, girl," Elizabeth said as she offered Goody Two-shoes an apple.

The horse daintily took the apple from Elizabeth's hand. "Good girl," she said, stroking the horse's muzzle.

Just then one of the Handel boys came running around the corner. Elizabeth checked the shoes. Nikes. It was Chris.

Elizabeth sighed. Here was the boy of her dreams, and he was probably going to ask her where Jessica was.

"Uh . . . ," he said blankly as he stared at Elizabeth. "I hate to ask you this after everything we talked about last night, but . . . which one are you? Jessica or Elizabeth?"

Elizabeth felt her heart pound. *I shouldn't do this,* she thought.

But I have to.

She backed away from Goody Two-shoes's stall and gave Sleepy, who was in the next stall over, a pat. "I'm Jessica," she said, hoping she sounded more confident than she felt.

"Oh," Chris said vacantly. "OK. Good."

Was that disappointment I heard in his voice? Elizabeth wondered. *Was he actually wishing I was Elizabeth?*

No, you're imagining things, she told herself.

As Chris stepped closer to her Elizabeth slid her long-sleeved shirt down over her watch. Her heart beat faster with each step closer he took.

"We've got some time to kill before the trail ride," Chris said. His green eyes sparkled even in the dim light of the barn. "Would you like to take a walk?"

"Oh, yes!" Elizabeth said eagerly.

"Come on, then," he said, motioning her to follow.

Elizabeth sighed. *I can't believe I'm doing this,* she thought. *This is terribly wrong.* But she couldn't help herself. She followed him out of the barn.

"What's your cheering squad like?" Chris asked as they strolled along the paddock. "Is it fun to be on it?"

"Um, yeah," Elizabeth said nervously. She tried to think of something interesting Jessica had said about the Boosters recently. "Let's see. We sold candy a while back to raise money for new uniforms."

"That's nice," Chris replied. "What color are your new uniforms going to be?"

What color? Elizabeth had no idea. This was a mess. Not only was she stealing her sister's boyfriend, but she was lying to the guy she really liked.

"Are they blue?" Chris persisted. "Blue is my favorite color."

Elizabeth's heart leaped. "Blue is my favorite color too!" she blurted.

But it wasn't Jessica's favorite color. Jessica's favorite color was pink.

"Really!" Chris said, grinning at her.

Elizabeth couldn't even look at him anymore. She felt like such a fake. A boyfriend-stealing fake.

But as she turned away from Chris, Elizabeth caught a glimpse of something out of the corner of her eye.

Not something, she realized. Someone. *Jessica!* She was leaning against the paddock fence with her back to Elizabeth. And Nick was right beside her.

Elizabeth crossed her arms. *Well*, she thought angrily. *It seems I'm not the only boyfriend stealer here.*

Chris nudged her. "Hey, there's your sister and my brother," he said cheerfully. "Hey, Nick, Elizabeth." Chris waved to them. "It looks like you guys had the same idea we had. Taking a walk before the trail ride."

Jessica whirled around. Her jaw dropped when she saw Elizabeth.

"Hi, Jessica." Nick waved to Elizabeth.

"Hi." Elizabeth forced a smile as she waved back. It wasn't easy to smile at Nick while glaring at Jessica, who was standing right beside him.

"I, uh, forgot something back in the room," Jessica said suddenly as she threw a murderous look at Elizabeth. Then she grabbed Nick's hand. "Will you excuse me?" she asked sweetly.

"Sure, Elizabeth," he replied. "I'll see you at the trail ride."

So I'm not the only *imposter here!* Elizabeth realized. "I think I forgot something too," Elizabeth told Chris. "Can I catch you later?"

"OK, Jessica," Chris responded, looking puzzled.

"Wait up, Elizabeth!" Elizabeth called to Jessica.

"Sure, Jessica," Jessica replied. Elizabeth could see her twin was every bit as angry as she was.

"How dare you!" Jessica exploded as soon as they reached their cabin. "How dare you go after Chris behind my back!"

"Oh, like you weren't going after Nick behind *my* back," Elizabeth shouted back, folding her arms across her chest. "Traitor!"

"Cheater!" Jessica screamed.

"Boyfriend stealer!" Elizabeth screamed right back.

The girls stood eye to eye and nose to nose, glaring at each other. Until suddenly they both burst out laughing.

"Jessica," Elizabeth said between giggles, "let me get this straight. We were each pretending to be each other—"

"—just so we could be with the guy we really liked!" Jessica finished the sentence, and they both collapsed with laughter.

"And the whole time," Elizabeth said, wiping away a tear, "I was afraid to tell you to your face because I didn't want to hurt your feelings."

"Me too!" Jessica said. "This is so perfect. You like Chris and I like Nick."

Elizabeth's forehead wrinkled with concern. "Yeah, that's great for us. But how do we tell *them* without hurting *their* feelings?"

Jessica flopped down on her bed. "Good point," she said, sighing heavily. "I can't just tell Chris I'd rather be with Nick, and you can't just tell Nick you'd rather be with Chris."

"What are we going to do?" Elizabeth moaned as she flopped down beside Jessica.

Jessica thought about it for a few minutes. Then she bolted up. "I've got it!" she exclaimed.

"What?" Elizabeth asked, raising herself up onto her elbows.

"I don't know about you, but I had Nick totally convinced I was you," Jessica informed her sister.

A slow smile spread across Elizabeth's face. "And I had Chris totally convinced I was you!" she added, sitting all the way up.

"Are you thinking what I'm thinking?" Jessica asked, her eyes twinkling with excitement.

Elizabeth nodded. "As long as we both agree, what's the harm? Let's do it," she said, snapping her fingers. "Let's switch places for the rest of the trip."

"Maybe even the rest of our lives," Jessica said seriously. "If things work out right."

Eight

◇

I don't know how Elizabeth can stand these stupid barrettes, Jessica thought as she and Nick strolled around the pond later that evening.

She'd been wearing Elizabeth's barrettes for most of the day now, and they were giving her a terrible headache. *Well, I'm just going to have to get used to it,* she told herself. *Just like I'm going to have to get used to toning down my naturally great fashion sense,* she thought scornfully as she looked at the peasant skirt she was wearing.

The things I'm willing to do for love!

The sun was just starting to sink below the horizon. It cast a fiery glow onto the pond. Jessica was proud of herself for noticing that. It was the sort of thing Elizabeth would notice.

Of course, Jessica had lots of time to notice

things like that because Nick was hardly doing any talking. He hadn't asked her any questions about herself. Er, about Elizabeth. And he certainly hadn't volunteered much about himself either. He was busy looking down at his Reebok sneakers.

Jessica was getting tired of the silence. "I've been thinking about writing an article for our school newspaper about our trip here," she said, trying to make conversation.

Nick smiled at her. "That's nice," he responded.

"Uh, yeah," she said brightly. "I was thinking I'd write about the beautiful scenery along the trail." That was something Elizabeth would say, wasn't it?

"Yeah, it is pretty up here," Nick agreed, glancing around him.

Jessica sighed. She wished Nick would say something. *What's with him tonight anyway?* she wondered. *He was so much fun last night.*

"Well, why don't you tell me more about your future movie career," Jessica said, trying again.

"What?" Nick said, scratching his head. "Oh. Well, what do you want to know?"

Good question. What should she want to know? What would Elizabeth want to know? "Well, what kind of movies do you want to make?"

"Good ones," Nick responded. "I mean, funny ones."

"I like funny movies," Jessica offered.

"So do I," Nick said matter-of-factly.

This conversation is going nowhere fast, Jessica realized. *I just hope Elizabeth is having a better time than I am.*

"I really like math," Chris said enthusiastically.

Elizabeth paused. "I, uh, like math too," she said. Her favorite subject was really English, but she knew Jessica preferred math.

"Yeah, I especially like story problems," Chris went on. "You know, if train A travels at such and such speed and train B travels at such and such speed, at what point will they meet?"

"Uh, I don't think we've gotten to that yet," Elizabeth told him.

"Oh," Chris responded in a high-pitched voice. He cleared his throat. "Actually, neither have we. I just like math so much that I do it in my spare time."

"I see," Elizabeth answered.

As they walked, Chris seemed to be inching farther ahead of her. That was because she was having a hard time walking on Jessica's platform shoes. She knew it was just a matter of time before—

"Oh!" she gasped as her body pitched forward.

Luckily Chris caught her before she fell. "Are you OK?" he asked worriedly.

"Yeah," she said, smiling weakly as she regained her balance. "New shoes," she explained.

Chris scratched his head. "Gee, they don't look that new," he said.

"Uh, well, I bought them at a thrift shop," Elizabeth said quickly.

But Jessica would never buy anything at a thrift shop, Elizabeth reminded herself. *I hope Chris doesn't know us well enough yet to realize that.*

"Thrift shops are good," Chris said eagerly. "I mean, isn't it great to walk into one, pick something out, and then think about how much money you saved? For instance, I bet those shoes cost at least twenty-five bucks new. But what did you pay for them? Probably no more than five. That's a savings of, what? Lots more than fifty percent."

Math again? Elizabeth thought.

"See what I mean about math?" Chris said as though he were reading her mind. "I just can't keep myself from doing it."

Elizabeth forced a smile. She had thought that once she and Jessica switched places, everything would be great. She'd be with Chris and Jessica would be with Nick. But for some reason things seemed more awkward than ever.

"Quit laughing," Elizabeth ordered her twin. The two were in the bathroom, brushing their teeth later that night. Elizabeth was telling Jessica about her evening with Chris.

"I'm sorry." Jessica giggled. A blob of toothpaste

was stuck to her cheek. "I do like math, but obviously not as much as Chris does. I think we were right to switch places."

"So you had a good time with Nick?" Elizabeth asked curiously.

"Well." Jessica hesitated, turning off the water. "Not really. I mean, no matter what we talked about, the conversation just sort of fizzled out."

"I don't know what went wrong tonight," Elizabeth said as she put on her nightshirt.

"Well, whatever it was, the boys noticed it too," Jessica declared. "Did you hear how Nick said good night to me? He said, 'Bye, Elizabeth. I mean, Jessica. No, Elizabeth!' It was like he didn't even know who I was."

Elizabeth looked worried. "Do you think they know we switched?"

"Nah," Jessica said, burying her face in her towel. "How could they?"

Elizabeth juggled her hairbrush from hand to hand absently. *If they didn't know, why was the evening such a disaster?* Elizabeth wondered. As she brushed her hair she replayed all the events of the evening from the moment the boys met them in the dining hall until Chris's final good-bye.

"That's it!" she exclaimed suddenly, banging her fist on the bathroom counter.

"What?" Jessica asked, her forehead wrinkling with confusion.

Elizabeth turned to her sister. "When Chris said good night to me, he waved . . . *with his left hand!*"

"So?" Jessica frowned.

"Don't you get it?" Elizabeth exclaimed. She felt like Christine Davenport, the heroine in her Amanda Howard mysteries. "Chris is *right-handed*. He wouldn't have waved with his left hand. The boys must have switched places too!"

"Of all the low-down dirty tricks—" Jessica scowled as she folded her arms across her chest.

"Jessica! It's the exact same thing we did," Elizabeth reminded her twin.

"Yeah, but since they did it too that just puts us right back where we started. You're still with Nick, and I'm still with Chris," Jessica grumbled. "They ruined everything!"

"Well, they obviously felt the same way we did," Elizabeth said reasonably. "They wanted to switch partners too."

"Yeah, but what do we do now?" Jessica asked. She sighed heavily as she sank to the floor and rested her head on her knees. "We're back with the wrong guys again."

"Well, I think the solution is simple." Elizabeth shrugged. "We just go back to being ourselves."

A smile spread slowly across Jessica's face. "So you'll actually be with Chris, even though he's pretending to be Nick. And I'll actually be with Nick, even though he's pretending to be Chris."

"Yeah." Elizabeth blinked. "I guess." For some reason it didn't seem quite so simple when Jessica said it out loud. But as she massaged her aching feet, all she could think about was how happy she was that she could go back to being herself. She didn't think she could handle another night on Jessica's platform shoes. "But what if they decide to switch back too, Jess?"

"Don't worry, Lizzie," Jessica said, misreading Elizabeth's concern. "We'll get things straightened out. We'll each get with the right guy."

Elizabeth winced as her fingers traveled over the blister on her big toe. "I hope so," she said. "I don't think my feet can take much more of this."

"Good morning!" the Handel twins greeted Jessica and Elizabeth in the stable the next morning.

Jessica checked their shoes. "Hi, Chris." She hoped the twin in the Nike sneakers was really Nick.

"Hi, Nick," Elizabeth said to the boy in Reebok sneakers as she rubbed Goody Two-shoes's nose.

The Handels glanced at each other. "You guys are pretty good at figuring out which of us is which," the boy in the Nike sneakers—*Nick-as-Chris,* Jessica thought confidently—remarked.

Jessica flipped her hair over her shoulder and giggled nervously. "I told you that you can't fool twins," she said, wagging her finger at them. "Now, which of us is which?"

The boy in the Reebok sneakers—Chris-as-Nick—grabbed his brother's arm. "Do you remember which of them said you can't fool twins?" he asked in a teasing voice.

"Sure," Nick-as-Chris responded with a straight face. "Elizabeth did."

"Excuse me?" Jessica planted a hand on her hip and raised her eyebrow. *Way to blow your cover, Jessica*, she thought.

The boy in the Nike sneakers laughed. "I'm kidding. I know it was you who said that, Jessica."

"Sure you did, Chris." Jessica sniffed. "Easy for you to say. You tricked me."

"I did not," Nick-as-Chris insisted. "I already knew which twin you were."

"Oh, yeah? Prove it!" Jessica challenged playfully.

"Easy. Elizabeth is the one over there petting Goody Two-shoes," Nick said triumphantly.

Jessica wasn't ready to let him off the hook so easily. "That doesn't mean anything," she informed him. "We still could've switched." Jessica winked at her sister, who grinned and turned away. "Maybe I'm really Elizabeth and Jessica is just petting Goody Two-shoes to throw you guys off," Jessica went on.

"I doubt it," Nick-as-Chris teased.

To prove her point, Jessica went over to the horse and reached up to pet him on the other side. But as she did the horse snorted and took a step back.

Everyone but Jessica laughed.

"Face it, Jess," Elizabeth said. "Nick—uh, *Chris* got you there. For some reason this horse just doesn't like you."

"Yup. You'll never be able to fool us now," Nick-as-Chris said as he stepped toward Jessica.

Jessica and Elizabeth exchanged looks of relief. *I hope we won't have to fool the Handels anymore,* Jessica thought, getting away from the horse as quickly as she could.

Steven couldn't believe his rotten luck. This horse was so slow! "Do you have lead in your hooves or what?" Steven asked Rocket.

The horse just plodded on, unaware of Steven's annoyance.

Way in the distance Steven could see his sisters with those twin boys they liked. The four of them had lagged behind everyone else, talking and flirting among themselves. If those four were that far ahead of him, Steven could only imagine how far the rest of the group was.

"I should never have paid any attention to that guy who talked about your California Derby days," Steven grumbled. "I mean, I knew he was talking about a while ago, but just how long ago was it? A hundred years?"

No response. The only sound Steven heard was the steady *clomp, clomp* of Rocket's hooves against the hard dirt trail. And an occasional snort.

Steven sighed. *Some vacation,* he thought miserably.

"What are you doing? Buying out the store?" one of the Handel boys asked.

Jessica was in the gift shop. She had a stack of Triple Z Ranch shirts in one hand and her father's credit card in the other.

"Let me help you with those," he offered, taking several of the shirts from her pile.

"Thanks," Jessica said. She glanced down at the boy's feet. Reebok sneakers. Which meant Nick. But since the boys had switched places, it had to be Chris, who was pretending to be Nick. Darn!

"Jessica? Right?" Chris-as-Nick asked.

"Yup." Jessica nodded. She didn't think it was even worth asking which twin he was. He'd say he was Nick, but Jessica knew the truth.

"I hear our families are having dinner together in town tonight," Chris-as-Nick said as he placed the stack of shirts on the counter.

Yeah, and this time you can cut Lizzie's *Jell-O up into a thousand little pieces*, Jessica thought as she placed the rest of her shirts on the counter. She handed the cashier her dad's credit card, then turned back to Chris-as-Nick. "Uh, yeah," she said. "Lizzie and I are really excited about it."

"So are we." The boy smiled. "Well, I guess I'll see you at dinner."

"For sure," Jessica said cheerfully.

Once he was gone, Jessica rolled her eyes. She sure was glad she and Lizzie had figured out that the boys had switched places too. Maybe tonight they could all finally have a good time together.

Nine

"So what exactly is a buffalo burger, Chris?" Jessica asked, glancing up from her menu. "Is it kind of like buffalo wings?"

"No," he replied, laughing. "First of all, buffalo wings are really chicken wings."

"Duh," Jessica responded, rolling her eyes at Chris, er, the boy who called himself Chris. Jessica knew he was really Nick. And Nick was really Chris. That was why Jessica sat down across from the boy in Nike sneakers and Elizabeth sat down across from the boy in Reebok sneakers.

"They must call them buffalo wings for a reason," Jessica remarked, flipping her hair behind her shoulder. "Don't they taste sort of like buffalo meat?"

The Handels looked at each other. "Not really," Nick responded.

"Buffalo meat is hard to describe," Chris added. "You'll just have to try it."

"Whatever it is, I'm sure it's good," Elizabeth assured Jessica. "Mr. and Mrs. Hogan wouldn't have insisted we all come here otherwise."

The Wakefields, the Hogans, and several other guests from the Triple Z Ranch had come into town to have dinner at Sally's Saloon. Sally's Saloon was known all over the area for its buffalo burgers and its down-home after-dinner entertainment.

Jessica and Elizabeth had put on their nicest dresses for the occasion. Jessica was wearing her new pink minidress, and Elizabeth was wearing a blue chambray pioneer dress that buttoned all the way up to her neck. Even though their parents were in the same restaurant, the girls had managed to talk them into letting them eat with Nick and Chris. Alone.

"All right." Jessica closed her menu. "I'll try it too. But it better be good!"

"It will be," Nick-as-Chris promised.

"So, have you guys been to many dude ranches before?" Jessica asked, leaning back against the hard wooden booth.

Chris-as-Nick shook his head. "Nope. This is our first time."

"Really?" Elizabeth looked surprised. "You guys both seem to know a lot about horses."

"Well, we've certainly been riding before," Nick-as-Chris explained. "There are several stables near Merrill Falls."

"Yeah, we even took riding lessons last summer," Chris-as-Nick added.

"No, I took riding lessons last summer," Nick-as-Chris said, jamming his thumb to his chest. "You just sat on your horse with your camera and filmed everyone else."

Chris-as-Nick nudged his brother, pretending to be annoyed.

Jessica did a double take. Wasn't Nick the one who wanted to make movies? And wasn't the Nick across from Elizabeth really Chris?

Did they switch back again?

Of course not, Jessica told herself. Chris probably just said that to make sure Jessica and Elizabeth didn't catch on to the fact they'd switched identities. *Pretty sneaky,* Jessica thought, folding her arms across her chest. *Too bad we're not as gullible as you guys think we are.*

"I've got your salads here," the waitress said, balancing a round tray on her shoulder.

"Great!" Nick-as-Chris said, picking up his fork. "I'm starving."

Jessica noticed he was holding the fork in his right hand. *Way to make it believable,* she thought. But she was anxious to see Nick actually eat with his right hand.

"Can I get you anything else?" the waitress asked

as she set an assortment of salad dressings in the middle of the table.

"No, that'll be fine," Jessica said quickly. She picked up her fork. "Well, come on, you guys. Let's dig in!" She didn't take her eyes off of Nick-as-Chris's fork.

"Jessica?" Chris-as-Nick asked politely. "Would you pass the ranch dressing, please?"

"Huh?" She blinked. "Oh, sure. Here you go." She slid it over to Elizabeth, who passed it across the table to Chris-as-Nick.

"Aren't you going to eat?" Jessica asked Nick-as-Chris.

He looked at her and laughed. "I'd like to put some dressing on my salad first," he said as his twin brother passed him the ranch dressing.

"Well, you said you were hungry," Jessica pointed out. She popped a carrot into her mouth as she watched Nick-as-Chris ladle dressing onto his salad. With his right hand.

Suddenly Jessica felt Elizabeth's elbow in her ribs. Elizabeth tilted her head toward Chris-as-Nick, who was taking forkful after forkful of salad. With his left hand. And he didn't seem to be having any trouble at all. *If that really was Chris,* Jessica reasoned, *he'd be right-handed. No way could he switch hands so easily.*

So it's not just me, Jessica thought. *Elizabeth notices too.*

Jessica bit her lip as she looked at Elizabeth. This could only mean one thing. The boys switched back to themselves too! That really was Chris sitting across from her. And that really was Nick sitting across from Elizabeth.

They were back with the wrong guys again!

"What's the matter?" Chris-as-Chris asked, glancing from Elizabeth to Jessica. "How come neither of you is eating?"

"Uh, I have to go to the bathroom," Jessica said, wiping her mouth with her napkin. She grabbed her twin's arm. "And so does Elizabeth!"

"We'll be back in a minute." Elizabeth smiled weakly. "Don't move!"

Elizabeth put her hand over her mouth to stifle her giggles. "You have to admit, this is kind of funny."

"Funny?" Jessica cried as she paced back and forth in the small bathroom. She looked like a caged tiger about to strike. "Elizabeth, this is our future you're laughing about. If we don't get this right, we're doomed to spend the rest of our lives with the wrong guys."

"So what are we going to do now?" Elizabeth planted a hand on her hip. "Tell them?"

"Tell them!" Jessica exclaimed as though it were the most ridiculous thing she'd ever heard. "No way. We'll just . . . switch to plan C, that's all."

"And just what is plan C?" Elizabeth asked, raising her eyebrow.

Jessica frowned. "Well, since Nick really is Nick, and Chris really is Chris . . ." Suddenly she snapped her fingers. "We'll switch again," she said brightly. "Just like we did the first time. I'll be you, you'll be me, and we'll both be with the guys we like."

"So what you're saying is, plan C is the same as plan A," Elizabeth said skeptically. "Remember how well that one worked, Jess? Forget it."

"There's no time to argue, Lizzie," Jessica demanded. "We're switching. Right now. Quick! Take off your dress and give it to me. I'll give you mine." She kicked off her shoes and unzipped her dress.

Elizabeth could only stare at her dumbly. "You've got to be kidding," she said.

"I'm not," Jessica assured her. "Come on. It's the only way!"

"But we can't switch midway through our date!" Elizabeth objected.

"Sure, we can," Jessica said firmly as she eased the dress down past her hips.

Elizabeth glanced around the brightly lit bathroom. It was a one-stall bathroom and the door was locked, so it wasn't like anyone could come in and interrupt them. It was just, well, she had worn this dress especially for Chris. He said his favorite color was blue.

Elizabeth sighed heavily. She could end up with

the right guy and the wrong dress or the right dress and the wrong guy. Which was more important?

"I don't know what you're complaining about," Jessica said as she handed Elizabeth her dress. "You get to wear this cool minidress while I have to suffocate under all those buttons."

Elizabeth stared at the dress in her hands. *Cool is right*, she thought unhappily. *I'm going to freeze to death.*

But there was no time to argue. It was definitely better to end up with the right guy and the wrong dress. She and Jessica had to switch. Now.

Elizabeth pulled the barrettes out of her hair and began unbuttoning her dress.

When the twins finally came back out, the boys were just coming back to the table too. *Hmmm*, Jessica thought. *Where did they go?*

She took Elizabeth's seat as the boys slid into the booth. Jessica hoped she really was across from Nick this time.

"Oh, good! Our burgers are here!" Chris declared, picking his up.

Jessica frowned. How was she going to know for sure who was who if they weren't going to use their forks? "Uh, shouldn't we finish our salads before we dig into our burgers?" she asked, smiling brightly.

"Nah," Chris responded. "I'm not much for salad anyway."

"Yeah, what are you? Our mother?" Nick teased as he took a bite of his burger.

Jessica sighed. How else could she figure out who was who without coming right out and asking? Their shoes! *Chris wears Nike sneakers and Nick wears Reebok sneakers. So the person across from me should be wearing Reebok sneakers. And unless they changed clothes and shoes in the last five minutes, that person should be Nick.* She smiled to herself. *Ha! And everyone says Elizabeth is the smart twin,* she thought proudly.

Jessica carefully nudged her knife to the floor. "Oops," she said weakly.

"Oh, I'll get that!" Nick offered, leaning over.

"No!" Jessica cried. She lowered her voice. "I mean, I dropped it. I should get it."

She slid herself under the table and retrieved her knife. At the same time she glanced at the boys' shoes. It was dark, so it was kind of hard to tell. But she thought she saw the Nike stripe on Chris's foot. And Chris was sitting across from Elizabeth. So that was right. Wasn't it? Unless they switched shoes too.

Jessica crawled back up to the booth. "Got it!" she said, waving her knife in the air.

Nick smiled at her. "Good."

"Well, I see you like your burger, Jessica," Chris commented.

I do? Jessica thought. *But I haven't even taken a*

bite yet. Then she realized Chris was looking at Elizabeth.

"Yeah, it's pretty good," Elizabeth said uneasily as she glanced at Jessica out of the corner of her eye.

I'm Elizabeth, Jessica reminded herself. She picked up her own burger. *I'm Elizabeth and I actually like trying new foods,* she thought as she sniffed her burger. It kind of smelled like Thanksgiving dinner, but not really.

Jessica took a small nibble out of the side of her burger. But as she did, she saw Nick pick up his fork with his right hand and spear a leaf of lettuce with it. *Aha!* she thought. *They* did *switch. Just like we did. Time for us to switch back!*

Jessica nudged her sister. "I left something in the bathroom, Jess."

Elizabeth looked confused, then she seemed to understand. "Oh, right, Lizzie. You forgot—that—one—*thing.* We'd, uh, better go get it. Excuse us, guys."

"Don't you two go anywhere!" Jessica said as she and her twin sister darted for the bathroom.

Elizabeth sighed. "How can you be sure they switched too? You said yourself Nick only took one bite." The girls were back in the bathroom, arguing over whether or not they should switch back.

"Yes, but I saw Nick use his right hand," Jessica insisted. "He probably thought no one would notice just one bite. But I did. I'm telling you, they switched too. We've got to switch back."

Elizabeth sighed again as she kicked off Jessica's shoes and unzipped Jessica's dress. "All right, Jess. But this is the last time. I'm tired of all this switching back and forth. It's making me totally confused. I've forgotten who's supposed to be with whom out there, and I'm not sure if I care anymore either." She paused. "Besides, I'm sick of buttoning that dress. It really is a pain!"

"Boy, you guys sure have to go to the bathroom a lot," one of the Handel boys commented as Elizabeth sat down on the bench and slid over to make room for Jessica. By this time Elizabeth was so tired and confused, she didn't even try to guess which one was talking.

"Well, when we got back from that ride this afternoon, Elizabeth and I drank like a gallon of water each. Right, Elizabeth?" Jessica nudged her.

What? Am I myself again? I must be if Jessica is calling me that. "Uh, yeah," Elizabeth spoke up. "That's right." She unfolded another napkin and placed it in her lap.

The buffalo burgers and salads had been cleared away while Elizabeth and Jessica were gone, and they were replaced with small dessert plates. A platter of chocolate brownies sat in the middle of the table.

"You guys have *got* to try these things," the boy across from Elizabeth said as he picked up another gooey square from the platter and popped the whole thing into his mouth.

"How can they try them if you eat them all?" the other boy asked as he elbowed his brother.

At the moment Elizabeth didn't care whether she got a brownie or not. She was just relieved that the evening was almost over. She couldn't wait to get back to their cabin and get out of Jessica's uncomfortable heels. They were pinching her toes.

Wait a minute! If she was Elizabeth, what was she doing still wearing Jessica's shoes?

Elizabeth lifted the tablecloth and glanced down at her feet. She was still wearing Jessica's heels with her pioneer dress. And Jessica was wearing her granny boots with her minidress!

Great! she thought, wanting to crawl under the table and disappear. *Just great!*

Ten

"This is our last chance to get things right or the double wedding is off!" Jessica announced as she barged into the bathroom early the next morning.

Elizabeth was at the sink, washing her face. She looked up at Jessica from under her arm. "I can't go through another night like last night," she informed Jessica. "Changing clothes every ten minutes? That was totally ridiculous! We were lucky the guys didn't notice that we ended up in each other's shoes."

"I agree." Jessica nodded. "That's why today we're going to wear the same outfit and we're each going to carry a watch and a set of barrettes." She set the watches and barrettes on the counter beside Elizabeth.

Elizabeth dried her face with her towel. "You've

got to be kidding," she said, glancing first at the barrettes, then at Jessica.

"Nope." Jessica shook her head. "Now, I know what you're thinking. We're individuals. We never dress alike. But Lizzie, this is for a good cause," she said earnestly as she followed her twin back to their room. "These guys may be our destinies and we may never get together with them because we're too busy changing clothes."

Elizabeth grabbed a pair of jeans from her bottom drawer. "So, what do you have in mind now?" she asked warily.

"I'm glad you asked." Jessica grinned as she plopped down on Elizabeth's bed. "It's simple, really. We each wear our purple jeans and our plain white shirts. We each carry barrettes and a watch. Then we head down to the barn and spy on them. We figure out who is playing who and we accessorize accordingly."

Elizabeth bit her lip. "It could work," she agreed.

"It has to work!" Jessica corrected. "Otherwise we may never reach our destinies."

Jessica decided to watch the barn from the rear entrance. Nobody ever went in or out that way. It would be a perfect spot to watch for the Handels.

She carried her watch in one hand and her barrettes in the other. She was ready to play either part—Jessica or Elizabeth.

As she stood in the doorway, people came in to get saddles and boots. But then they left right away. No one ever even looked her way. Until Steven came into the barn.

Yikes! Jessica quickly ducked out of sight. She couldn't let Steven see her. He'd call her by name and ruin everything.

She backed slowly around the back of the barn. As she turned the corner she backed right into somebody. "Ahhhh!" she screamed.

It was one of the Handel boys. But which one?

"You scared me to death," Jessica said awkwardly as she brushed a stray hair off her face.

"Uh, sorry . . . Elizabeth," the boy responded.

Elizabeth! Jessica wasn't expecting one of the boys to call her by name first. Quick! Which boy is this?

Jessica glanced down at the boy's feet. Reebok sneakers. Chris.

Or was it Nick?

Jessica couldn't remember which one wore Reebok sneakers and which one wore Nike sneakers.

No, it was definitely Nick. Nick and Nike sneakers both started with *N.* If Nick was the one who wore Nike sneakers, it would've been easier to remember. And nothing about the Handel boys was easy.

"You are Elizabeth, aren't you?" Nick asked cautiously.

Jessica put on her best smile. "That depends," she said mysteriously. "Are you Nick?"

The boy took a step closer. "Yup," he replied. "And I've been looking all over for Elizabeth."

Oh! Jessica's heart gave a leap. "Well, in that case, the answer is yes," she said flirtatiously, fiddling with the barrettes. "I was just fixing my hair."

This week has gone by so quickly, Elizabeth thought as she descended the hill leading to the stables. She could hardly believe this was her last day to ride Goody Two-shoes. She would definitely have to make time to go riding again once she got back to Sweet Valley.

As she approached the corral Elizabeth spotted one of the Handel boys. He was leaning against the fence, gazing off in the distance. *Which one is he?* Elizabeth wondered as she ran her fingers through her hair.

She was wearing her barrettes and her watch. She hoped that was OK.

But just then she caught a glimpse of her twin with the other Handel boy way at the far end of the barn. Jessica was wearing her barrettes. And she looked really happy.

Elizabeth sighed. *I guess I don't get to play myself today*, she thought as she pulled the barrettes out of her hair and stuffed them into her front jeans pocket.

She turned to the boy who was leaning against the fence. *I sure hope you're Chris*, Elizabeth thought as she approached him.

*   *   *

"Remember, folks," Mr. Hogan said. "This is our last ride. And we here at the Triple Z Ranch have a tradition at the end of our last ride."

Steven groaned as he thought about the cowboy hat he had absolutely no chance of winning.

"We'll all stop at that clearing about a mile from the ranch," Mr. Hogan went on. "Then those who want to can compete in a friendly little race back to the stables. The winner will receive a genuine Triple Z cowboy hat just like the one I'm wearing." He lifted his hat to show them.

"All right!" several of the riders cheered.

"Maybe they'll give you a head start," Mr. Wakefield teased Steven.

"Very funny, Dad," Steven grumbled. "Maybe you'd like to trade horses for the day."

"I don't think so, son." Mr. Wakefield shook his head. "I actually have my eye on that cowboy hat myself."

Steven ground his foot into the dirt. "Yeah, well, don't expect me to wish you luck."

"Here you go, Steven," Andy said, leading Rocket to him. "She's all set."

Is it my imagination or is that horse moving even slower today? Steven wondered. But he tried not to let his disappointment show as he accepted the reins.

Andy slapped Steven on the back. "I just want you to know I think you've been a great sport about this," he said. "I think it's been good for Rocket to get out on the trail this week."

Steven forced a smile. *Just call me Steven Wakefield, horse therapist.*

"Come on, Elizabeth, Nick. They're saddling your horses."

Jessica jumped when she heard her mother's voice. Uh-oh. The jig was up. She and Elizabeth could fool a couple of boys they'd never met before, but they certainly couldn't fool their own mother.

"Elizabeth?" Mrs. Wakefield squinted at Jessica. "Are you coming, dear?"

"Yeah, we're coming," Nick said, nudging Jessica.

Mrs. Wakefield smiled. "Good. I know you wouldn't want to miss a moment of your ride since today's the last day."

Jessica stared at her mother in amazement. Didn't she know? Didn't she even recognize her own daughter?

Oh, this is so great! Jessica thought as followed her mother through the barn. She could hardly wait to tell Elizabeth. *She'll never believe it. She'll never believe we actually fooled Mom!*

"Here you go, miss," Mr. Hogan said, handing her the reins.

Jessica's heart dropped.

"B-B-But this is Goody Two-shoes," she stammered.

Mr. Hogan looked confused. "Isn't she the horse you've been riding all week?"

"Oh. Yeah." Jessica forced a laugh. "I just thought that on the last day we were supposed to ride different horses."

"No." Mr. Hogan scratched his head. "We always assign horses on the first day and our guests keep those assignments for their entire stay."

"My mistake," Jessica muttered. *My funeral too,* she thought.

Eleven

Oh, no! Elizabeth could hardly believe her eyes. Jessica was leading Goody Two-shoes out of the barn!

Well, of course she is, Elizabeth told herself. *She's supposed to be you. And you're supposed to be her.*

Elizabeth's heart raced. This was a terrible mistake.

"Je—uh, Elizabeth!" Elizabeth screamed, running toward her twin. "Elizabeth!"

Jessica was with Nick, so that explained why she was smiling. But Elizabeth could see the worry in her sister's eyes.

"Um, I was wondering whether you'd like to trade horses today?" Elizabeth said cheerfully.

"With you?" Nick said, staring at Elizabeth.

"Of course with me!" Elizabeth frowned. "Who else?"

"Well, no offense, Jessica," Nick said, laughing.

"But you're not exactly Goody Two-shoes's favorite person."

"Oh, I think she's gotten used to me." Elizabeth laughed nervously. "See?" She reached up to stroke Goody Two-shoes's muzzle. The horse nickered and swished her tail from side to side.

"Still," Chris said, joining them. "I'd hate for anything bad to happen. I think you should let Elizabeth ride her."

"Yeah, Jess," Jessica said weakly. "You'd better let me ride her."

"No, really," Elizabeth insisted. "I want to prove to myself and everyone else that I can handle this horse."

"We really prefer it if our guests stick with the same horse for their entire stay," Mr. Hogan said as he led Chris's horse over to them.

Jessica cleared her throat. "Yeah, Jessica," she said, standing up a little taller. "This is my horse, so back off."

Jessica was actually insisting on riding Goody Two-shoes! Elizabeth gave her sister a hard look.

"Don't worry, I can handle it," Jessica whispered in Elizabeth's ear.

Elizabeth sighed. *I hope you can, Jess,* she thought, giving Goody Two-shoes one last rub. *I hope you can.*

I am *Elizabeth,* Jessica told herself. "I am Elizabeth," she told Goody Two-shoes as she swung her leg over the horse's back.

The horse bobbed her head, but Jessica seriously doubted the horse was nodding. *More likely she's trying to buck me off again,* Jessica thought.

"Now, we're just going to ride along nice and easy," Jessica whispered as she stroked Goody Two-shoes's mane. The horse could probably feel Jessica's pounding heart against her as Jessica leaned forward. But Jessica couldn't help that.

"I'll just sit here nice and still and you won't buck me off," Jessica whispered. "Have we got a deal?"

"You really like that horse, don't you?" Nick smiled. He had steered his horse, Easy Rider, over to her.

Jessica forced a smile. "I just love her," she gushed. *Did you hear that, Goody Two-shoes?*

"I can't believe Jessica wanted to take her away from you on the very last day," Nick went on.

"I don't know what she was thinking," Jessica responded, laughing nervously.

Goody Two-shoes stomped her front hoof and snorted.

Easy, Jessica thought with alarm. *Easy, girl!*

"It looks like she got nervous just having Jessica over here," Nick commented.

"Boy, isn't that weird?" Jessica responded.

Stupid horse! I can fool my own mother into thinking I'm Elizabeth, but why can't I fool you?

"Why do you keep turning around?" Chris asked

Elizabeth. They were riding side by side along the dusty trail. Jessica and Nick were a few hundred feet back.

"I, uh, didn't realize I was," Elizabeth lied as she turned back to Chris.

But she couldn't help worrying about Jessica. Goody Two-shoes had reared up on her at the beginning of the week. And Jessica really didn't have all that much experience with horses.

"I think I know what's going on," Chris said in a serious voice.

Elizabeth's stomach dropped. "You do?" she said weakly. In a sense, it was almost a relief. She didn't have to pretend anymore. She could be herself again.

"I can see how much your riding has improved over the week, Jessica," Chris said sincerely. He looked at her with sympathy. "And you want to try a more challenging horse than Sleepy, don't you?"

Elizabeth sighed. He didn't know after all! "Uh, yeah," she said quickly. "That's it."

"Well, maybe when we stop for a break, you and I can talk to Mr. Hogan," Chris suggested, shading his eyes from the bright sun. "Tell him what you just told me. Maybe he'll let you and me switch horses just for the final leg."

Elizabeth gazed at Chris. "You'd really do that for me?" she asked.

He nodded.

He's so sweet! Elizabeth thought. "OK. Let's talk to Mr. Hogan," she agreed. Then she glanced over her shoulder once again to check on her sister.

"Oh, the old gray mare, she ain't what she used to be," Steven sang. "Ain't what she used to be. Ain't what she used to be. The old gray mare, she ain't what she used to be. Many long years ago."

Steven didn't have to worry about what anybody thought of his singing. He was so far behind the rest of the group, no one could possibly hear him.

"I'm not asking you to enter the race or anything," Steven told Rocket. "I mean, who needs a dumb old cowboy hat, right?"

No response. Not that Steven actually expected a response. He didn't expect much of anything from this horse anymore.

"It would be nice if we could get back to the ranch before dark, though," Steven told Rocket. "Do you think you could manage that?"

The horse just plodded on. *Clip. Clop. Clip. Clop.*

Steven sighed. "I know you're old and everything. But come on. Doesn't it bother you that you're supposed to be this great racehorse and every animal here can run circles around you?"

Clip. Clop. Clip. Clop.

"None of these other horses have ever been to the California Derby," Steven pointed out.

Clip. Clop. Clip. Clop.

"Don't you have any pride at all?"

Clip. Clop. Clip. Clop.

I guess not, Steven thought. *And by the time this ride is over, I won't have any left either.*

"Elizabeth? Are you listening?" Nick asked.

"Huh?" Jessica whirled around to face Nick. But as she did, she almost slipped off her horse. "Whoa!" she shrieked, grabbing the saddle horn.

Dumb old horse. It seemed like Goody Two-shoes was doing everything she could to force Jessica off her back. But so far it hadn't worked. *That's because deep down, I'm every bit as good a rider as Elizabeth,* Jessica thought smugly.

"Gee, Elizabeth," Nick said, scratching his head. "You just don't seem like yourself today. I keep calling your name, but you don't even hear me."

Jessica settled herself in her saddle again. "W-W-What do you mean?" she asked nervously. She'd stayed on the horse, hadn't she? Jessica thought she was doing a pretty good job of being Elizabeth. Considering the fact that she was scared to death.

"You just seem . . . I don't know . . . distracted," Nick declared.

You'd be distracted too if you had to deal with a wild horse like this, Jessica thought.

Nick went on talking about some movie he wanted to make one day, and Jessica did her best to control her horse, who was pawing at the ground. Jessica squeezed her legs against the horse's sides and held tight to the saddle horn.

"Howdy there, kids," Mr. Hogan said, pulling up beside Nick.

Jessica grabbed her horse's reins. *Steady*, she thought. *There's plenty of room on this path for three horses.*

"Are you going to enter our little race today, Elizabeth?" Mr. Hogan said.

Jessica sat perfectly still in her saddle, keeping her eyes focused on the trail ahead. For the moment, everything was OK.

"Elizabeth?" Mr. Hogan repeated.

"Huh?" Jessica turned. She had heard Mr. Hogan; she just didn't realize he was talking to her. But of course he was. She was Elizabeth. Or at least everyone thought she was.

"I think you should consider racing. You're a terrific rider."

"Yeah, she's so good, she practically tunes out everything else around her," Nick muttered.

"That's because I just love horses!" Jessica exclaimed, eating up the praise. "I always have. It's like I have this sixth sense about horses. I can ride horses that no one else can."

"So does that mean you're going to race?" Nick asked, raising an eyebrow.

"I'll, uh, have to think about it," Jessica replied

as Goody Two-shoes lifted her head and snorted once more.

What could Mr. Hogan and Jessica be talking about? Elizabeth wondered as she watched them over her shoulder. They looked awfully serious.

Chris sighed. "Jessica! You're doing it again," he pointed out.

Elizabeth looked puzzled. "Doing what?"

"Watching your sister and my brother."

"Oh. Sorry," Elizabeth said, ashamed.

"Hey, kids," Mr. Hogan interrupted as he rode up behind them. "How are you doing?"

"Fine, Mr. Hogan," Elizabeth replied.

"We're going to rest for a while in the orchard up ahead," Mr. Hogan informed them. "Then those who want to can race back to the barn."

"OK. We'll see you in a few minutes," Chris said.

Elizabeth had kind of hoped she'd get a chance to race for that cowboy hat. But win a race on a horse named Sleepy? Not likely. Besides, horse racing wasn't something Jessica was likely to do.

Chris reached across for Elizabeth's hand. "I'm sorry if I'm being rude. It's just I was hoping this would be a chance for us to be together; you know, just the two of us. I really like you, Jessica."

Elizabeth felt a gentle stirring within her. She swallowed hard. "I, uh, like you too, Chris," she responded.

Her heart was pounding so hard, she thought it might explode. Was he going to kiss her? On horseback?

But the moment was broken by an earth-shattering scream. *"Help!"*

It's Jessica! Elizabeth realized.

She whirled around just as Goody Two-shoes reared up. Then suddenly Jessica was on the ground.

Twelve

Jessica's elbow hurt. But not as much as her pride.

"Elizabeth! Are you OK?" Nick jumped off his horse and ran over to her.

"I'm fine," Jessica said through gritted teeth as she grabbed a handful of dirt and threw it in the direction of Goody Two-shoes.

"Hey!" Nick cried, jumping out of the way. "Don't do that!"

"Why not?" Jessica asked, glaring at the horse. The stupid animal was standing there laughing at her. Jessica could see it in the beast's eyes.

Nick held out his hand and helped Jessica to her feet. He cocked his head and looked deep into her eyes. "You're not really Elizabeth, are you?" he said quietly.

"No, I'm Buffalo Bill," Jessica muttered, rubbing her elbow.

By this time Elizabeth and Chris had reached them. "What happened? Are you OK?" Elizabeth asked with concern.

But before Jessica could respond, Nick turned to Elizabeth. "So if she's not Elizabeth, then you must not be Jessica," he said, folding his arms across his chest.

Elizabeth looked at Jessica, then shook her head. "No, I'm not," she admitted.

Chris's jaw dropped. "You're not?" he asked, glancing from Jessica to Elizabeth.

Elizabeth shook her head and looked at the ground.

"You mean you guys switched places?" Chris asked, looking genuinely hurt. "Why would you try to fool us like that?"

Jessica rolled her eyes. "The same reason you guys were trying to fool us," she said indignantly.

Nick and Chris looked at each other in surprise.

"I don't know what you're talking about," Nick said.

"Yeah, we never tried to fool you," Chris put in. "We never switched places. We wouldn't ever do something like that."

"Yeah, right!" Jessica snorted. "Weren't you guys just saying how you'd fooled your own parents for a whole weekend?"

The boys looked at each other again. "We might try to fool our parents or our friends," Nick admitted. "But never our girlfriends."

Jessica looked at Elizabeth. Their eyes met and held. Was it possible they were telling the truth?

"I, uh, don't know what to say," Elizabeth said, ashamed. Her face was bright red. "We're really sorry."

"Yeah, well, you're obviously not the girls we thought you were," Nick said. He cuffed his brother on the arm. "Come on. Let's go."

Jessica watched as the boys got on their horses and rode away. "There go our destinies," she said with a sigh. "Riding off into the sunset."

"There you are!" Mr. Hogan called cheerfully as he rode toward Steven.

Steven groaned. *Everyone else must be even farther ahead than I thought.* Mr. Hogan looked like he'd been riding quite a while.

"You doing OK back here?" Mr. Hogan asked as he slowed his horse and turned her around.

"Sure." Steven shrugged. *It's not like you could get hurt going less than one mile an hour.*

"Good." Mr. Hogan grinned. "Listen, the reason I came back here was to see whether you'd mind if we went ahead with the final race without you." He looked at Steven expectantly.

"Mind? Why should I mind?" Steven asked flatly. *It's not like I have any chance of winning.*

Mr. Hogan breathed a sigh of relief. "Good. The other riders have been waiting at the clearing for quite a while already. They're pretty anxious to get this race under way."

Oh, sure, Steven thought. *Rub it in.*

"Well, I'll see you back at the stables, then," Mr. Hogan said. "And, uh, I'll have Andy or one of the other guys wait for you, OK?"

Steven tried not to look as annoyed as he felt. "Fine," he said through his teeth.

With that, Mr. Hogan clucked his tongue and his horse took off at a steady gallop.

"Now why can't you gallop like that?" Steven asked Rocket. "Does that really look so difficult?"

In response Rocket came to a complete stop.

Steven sighed. "I don't believe this," he muttered, swiping at a fly that buzzed near his ear. "I should just get off you and walk back to the stables. At least I'll get there yet this century."

Rocket snorted. She glanced over her shoulder and swished her tail. Then slowly, ever so slowly, she plodded on.

Jeez, I've had turtles that moved faster than this, Steven thought.

They went a few more feet, then Rocket stopped again.

"*Now what?*" Steven cried, throwing up his hands.

Rocket turned to the right. Steven heard the buzzing sound again. "It's a fly, Rocket," Steven said, totally exasperated. He squeezed his legs against the horse. "Now, come on! Let's *goooooooo!*"

Rocket let out a squeal, and Steven felt his body pitch backward. "Hey!" he cried, grabbing for the reins as Rocket took off at the speed of lightning.

"Whoa?" Steven cried, clinging to Rocket's mane. *"Whoa!"* He wasn't used to being on a horse that actually moved.

He shifted around in his saddle for better balance, then pulled back on the reins. "Come on! Slow down!" Steven said, feeling nervous. But the horse didn't pay any attention. She kept on running.

"It's certainly possible the Handels are telling the truth," Elizabeth said thoughtfully. She and Jessica were letting their horses move at their own leisurely pace. They weren't in any hurry to get back to the stables. They certainly weren't in any hurry to see the Handels again.

"I suppose," Jessica agreed. "But what about that first night we switched? Remember, you said Chris waved good-bye with his left hand."

"Yeah, but waving isn't really the same thing as writing or eating," Elizabeth pointed out. "I mean, can't you wave with your left hand as easily as you can with your right?"

Jessica put her left hand on her saddle horn as she waved with her right hand. Then she put her right hand on the saddle horn and she waved with her left hand. "I guess you're right," she admitted.

"But what about the next night when we were eating? I know I saw the guy who called himself Nick eating with his right hand, when he's supposed to be left-handed. And you saw the guy who called himself Chris eating with his left hand, when he should really be eating with his right."

"Yeah." Elizabeth let Goody Two-shoes meander off the path and over to some taller grass by the fence. "But think about Steven," she said as she grabbed the saddle horn and swung off the horse. "He's right-handed. But haven't you ever seen him eat a piece of meat? He holds his fork in his left hand and his knife in his right hand while he cuts his meat. But a lot of the time he doesn't bother to switch his fork back to his right hand."

Jessica snorted. "That's because Steven is a pig!"

Elizabeth patted her horse. "No. He just loves to eat."

"What about when they talked about the video camera?" Jessica asked. "Why would Chris use it if Nick is the one who's into movies?"

Elizabeth shrugged. "Why not?" she offered. "You've used a video camera before, haven't you? That's not proof of anything."

Jessica sighed. "So what you're saying is we don't have any real proof that the Handels ever switched places."

Elizabeth nodded. "That's exactly what I'm saying," she said softly. Elizabeth walked over to

Sleepy and held the horse's reins as Jessica shakily got out of the saddle.

"They must totally hate us," Jessica said, sitting down in the grass and shaking her head.

"Probably," Elizabeth agreed, kneeling next to her twin.

Jessica bit her lip. "I guess this means the double wedding is off."

"I know," Elizabeth admitted. "That's what I get for liking a boy more than a horse."

"Whooooaaaa! Whoa, girl, whoa, whoa, whoa!" Steven cried. No matter how hard he pulled on Rocket's reins or how loudly he yelled, he couldn't get the old horse to slow down.

Up ahead Steven spotted his sisters. They were sitting on the grass at the edge of the path. Their horses were grazing beside them. "Look out!" Steven shouted as Rocket sped toward them.

"What in the—" Jessica began. But Steven was already past her before she got the rest of her sentence out.

Steven and Rocket flew past the Handel boys, their parents, and several other riders. "Hey, isn't that that old racehorse?" one man asked another.

"Nah. Couldn't be," the other replied as Rocket zipped past.

Hold on! Steven told himself. *Just hold on! Rocket will tire out eventually.*

Rocket clomped through a grassy meadow. The horses in front of them were going pretty fast. But not as fast as Rocket. In just a few seconds Rocket had not only caught up to them but edged past.

"Rocket?" Mr. Hogan's eyes widened as Steven and Rocket zipped past.

The road veered off to the right, but Rocket barely slowed down. Steven could see the stables up ahead. And there were only three other riders in front of him.

This wasn't the race, was it? Steven wondered suddenly. Holding tight to the reins, he glanced over his shoulder. He hadn't noticed just how fast everyone else was going. "Ha, ha!" he cried out, raising his fist in the air. "This is the race! We're in the race, Rocket!"

Steven pressed his chest against Rocket's neck. "Come on, girl!" he shouted with excitement. "Go!"

"Steven!" Mr. Wakefield's eyes were wide with shock as Rocket tore past him.

"Sorry, Dad. Can't stay to chat," Steven called over his shoulder. "We've got a race to win!"

And they actually had a shot at winning! There was only one other rider ahead of them. "Here's your chance to show all these folks what you're made of," Steven whispered. "Come on! Let's win this thing!"

Rocket's hooves pounded the dirt road. *Clippity-clippity-clippity-clippity-clippity . . .*

"Ha, ha! We did it!" Steven cried with glee as they pulled ahead of the only other horse that was still in front of them. The stables were only about three hundred yards away now.

Two hundred yards.

One hundred yards.

The race was over. And Rocket had won!

"Phew!" Mr. Hillestad brought his horse to a stop beside Steven. "That was some mighty fine riding," he remarked as he took off his hat and wiped his brow.

"Yeah, I know," Steven panted. His chest was still heaving. This was the most exercise he'd gotten all week. "I should probably walk her a bit to cool her down, huh?"

"Probably should," Mr. Hillestad agreed as he swung his leg over the back of his horse and jumped down. "I haven't seen Rocket run like that in years."

By this time the other riders were coming in. "Well done, Steven," Mr. Handel complimented him.

"Now that's what I call coming from behind!" Mr. Hogan put in.

"That's for sure," Mr. Hillestad said, walking around behind the horse. "Take a look back here, Carl." He pointed to Rocket's rump.

Steven turned. "What?"

"Looks to me like old Rocket had a run-in with a bee," Mr. Hogan noted.

"Oh, no!" Steven gasped. He remembered the buzzing sound he'd heard. He had been sure it was a fly.

"Is she going to be all right?" Steven asked worriedly.

"Yeah, I'll just put some cream on her," Mr. Hillestad responded. "She'll be fine."

Steven dismounted Rocket so Mr. Hillestad could take her back to the barn.

"Well, son. It looks like you got that cowboy hat after all," Mr. Wakefield said, draping an arm over Steven's shoulders.

Steven cleared his throat. "Didn't I tell you I would?" he asked matter-of-factly. "All I needed was the right horse."

Thirteen

◇

"Are you ever going to take off that stupid cowboy hat?" Jessica asked Steven the next morning. The entire Wakefield family was out in the parking lot loading up the van.

"Sure," Steven replied. He took off the hat, plopped it onto Jessica's head, and then pushed it down over her eyes.

"Very funny," Jessica grumbled. She yanked off the hat and tossed it like a Frisbee toward the stables.

"Hey!" Steven cried, watching it roll down the hill. "You better go and get it."

Jessica grinned as she folded her arms across her chest. "Forget it. If you want it, you're going to have to go and get it yourself."

Steven sighed as the wind blew his hat a little

farther down the hill. "Yikes!" he cried, running after it.

"Serves you right for messing up my hair!" Jessica said, flipping her hair over her shoulder.

"Hey, Jess," Elizabeth whispered. She pointed toward the main building. "Look who's coming."

Jessica turned. The Handels!

"Do you think they're still mad?" Elizabeth whispered as Chris and Nick approached.

Jessica shrugged. "I don't know." She took a deep breath. "But here they come. Are you ready?"

"Ready as I'll ever be," Elizabeth replied.

The boys were wearing jeans and Triple Z Ranch T-shirts—the exact same thing Jessica and Elizabeth were wearing. It would have been impossible to tell the boys apart if the twins didn't already know that Chris wore Nike sneakers and Nick wore Reebok sneakers.

"Hello, Wakefield twins," one of the Handel boys greeted them. Nike sneakers. Chris.

"Hello," Elizabeth and Jessica responded in unison.

"I see you're both wearing your hair down and you're both wearing watches," Nick said, surveying the girls.

Jessica and Elizabeth glanced at each other. "We, uh, didn't really expect to see you guys," Elizabeth stammered. After all she and Jessica had been through with these guys, seeing them still made her heart race.

"We've decided to forgive you," Chris told them.

Elizabeth smiled. "I'm glad."

"Yeah. You know, we never meant to hurt anyone," Jessica put in.

"We know," Nick said. He reached out his hand. "Jessica, right?"

Elizabeth and Jessica looked at each other again and nodded. "Right," she said, waving a little at Nick. Her whole arm tingled.

"Do you still want to keep in touch, Jessica?" Nick asked as he led her slowly away from the van. He brought her to a spot by the fence where they could be alone. "I could give you my address."

"Oh, yes," she responded eagerly, and unzipped her backpack. "I'd really like that. Let me write down my address for you too." As she grabbed a pen and notepad her hand shook a little. *Why am I so nervous?* she asked herself. Then she smiled. *I must be with the right twin. If my hands are shaking, that means it's true love! I'm finally with the boy I liked all along!*

"Jessica?" Nick asked. As soon as she turned to look into his dazzling green eyes, Nick swung around and kissed her on the cheek.

Her jaw dropped open. She felt her cheeks burn. She just stared at him openmouthed, not knowing what to say.

Nick cleared his throat. "Are you going to give me your address or not, Jessica?"

"Uh, yeah," she said, shaking her head. She crouched down to use her knee as a table and quickly wrote her name and address on a page in her notepad. "Here you go," she said, tearing out the page and handing it to him. Then she handed him the pen and notepad. "Now you write down your address for me, Nick."

Nick scribbled something in the notepad and handed it back to her. "Write soon, OK, Jessica?" he said with a smile as he quickly turned and began walking away.

She sighed. All she wanted to do was lie down on the grass and remember getting that kiss over and over again. She glanced down at the notepad dreamily. And did a double take.

There, on her notepad, was written *Chris Handel*.

"Chris?" she called after him.

The boy turned around and gave her a wink. "You got it," he said, continuing on his way.

"No hard feelings, OK, Elizabeth?" Chris asked.

She leaned against the rear door of the van. Chris was looking into her eyes so intensely that she had to catch her breath before she could respond. "No hard feelings," she repeated, squinting in the sun. *This is* definitely *the right guy,* she thought. *I just know it. I can feel it!* "Look at those mountains, Chris. Aren't they beautiful? I'm really going to miss this place."

"Yeah," Chris said, running a hand through his curly dark hair. "You know what, Elizabeth? I'm going to miss you too."

"Really!" she squeaked, then caught herself. "Uh, I mean, *really?*" She blushed a little. *Calm down,* she told herself. *This is your big chance. Don't mess it up!* "And I—I—I'm going to miss you, Chris," she stammered.

Chris took two steps toward her, looked down at his Nike sneakers, then leaned over and kissed her on the cheek.

Wow! she thought, clasping her hand to her mouth. *I may never wash this cheek again.*

"I better go, Elizabeth," Chris said.

"Do you have to, Chris?" she asked with alarm, letting her fingers travel to the cheek he had just kissed.

Chris nodded. "Our folks are getting ready to leave."

She sighed. "OK. Well, good-bye, Chris," she said sadly.

"Good-bye, Elizabeth. By the way, I should let you in on a little secret," Chris said devilishly.

Her eyes widened. She held her breath before asking, "What is it?"

"I'm actually . . . *Ace Ventura! Pet detective!*" he blurted in a perfect Jim Carrey imitation.

She gasped. "Nick?"

The boy smiled, nodded, and gave her a wink before running back to his cabin.

*　　*　　*

"Elizabeth" was waiting impatiently by the minivan for her sister. She was smiling proudly to herself. *What a perfect plan,* she thought. *And it went without a hitch—for me at least.* She jumped up and down excitedly. She couldn't wait to find out if the plan worked for "Jessica" too.

"Hey, Lizzie!" she heard her twin call. "Jessica" was running toward her, waving her notepad in the air and bumping her backpack along behind her. She was alone. *All clear,* thought "Elizabeth"—who was actually Jessica.

"Don't 'Lizzie' me!" Jessica replied with a giggle. "We can be ourselves now. The coast is clear!"

"OK, Jess!" Elizabeth said. "So did you find out—"

"—that they switched on us?" Jessica finished.

"*Yes!*" they both screamed simultaneously.

"And did they figure out—" Elizabeth started.

"—that *we* actually switched on *them* too?" Jessica interrupted.

"*No!*" they both cheered at the same time.

"And did Chris—" Elizabeth touched her cheek.

"You mean Nick," Jessica interrupted. "And *yes!*" She nodded vigorously. "Did Nick—I mean, Chris . . . ?"

Elizabeth nodded, beaming happily.

The twins grabbed arms and danced with glee around the minivan.

"What happened?" Steven asked as he came

around to their side of the van. "Did you two just get out of the loony bin?"

That only made the twins laugh harder. Steven plopped his cowboy hat on his head and walked away. "Girls!" he muttered, shaking his head.

Once the twins had gotten their laughter under control, they just stood there and stared at each other. "Well done, *Jess*," Jessica told Elizabeth with a giggle.

Elizabeth grinned. "Way to go, *Lizzie*," she spouted back, slapping Jessica on the arm. "Boy, they sure thought they were fooling us. I wonder if they'll ever know that *we* got the last laugh." She climbed into the van, and Jessica climbed in after her. "So, Jess," Elizabeth continued, "how did you know that the Handel twins were switching on us just now?"

"What can I say?" Jessica bragged. "I'm Elizabeth. I'm the one with the brains here," she joked. "And besides, you know what they say about liars. It goes for twins too."

"What's that, Jess?" Elizabeth asked.

Jessica smiled mysteriously. "It takes one to know one."

"They were definitely the two cutest guys in the world, but Nick was even cuter than Chris!" Jessica was sitting in the Unicorner, where all the members of the Unicorn Club ate lunch. It was the first school day after winter break, and she was telling all her friends about her vacation. "I *always* knew which twin was Nick. There was something really special between us."

"Wow," Ellen Riteman said. "That sounds so romantic!"

"Oh, it was," Jessica declared. "Speaking of romance, why don't you tell us about *your* winter break, Lila?"

"I have something even better to tell you guys," Lila announced. "Have you heard who's coming to Sweet Valley? *Dr. Q.!*"

"The famous hypnotist?" Jessica squealed. "Cool!"

"And guess what else?" Lila continued. "I heard he might do a show here at school!"

What will happen when Dr. Q. comes to Sweet Valley? Find out in Sweet Valley Twins #102, **THE MYSTERIOUS DR. Q.**

Bantam Books in the SWEET VALLEY TWINS series.
Ask your bookseller for the books you have missed.

Cool stuff for you and your best friend!

We hope you enjoyed *Twins in Love*. Your opinion is important to us, and we'd love to hear from you. If you are one of the first 100 readers to return this questionnaire, we'll send you this cool stuff (one for you, one for your best friend).

• 2 Stuff Sacks

• 2 copies of magazine

• 2 autographed books

1. Did you like this book? (Check one) ⊘ I loved it   ○ I liked it   ○ It was OK
   ○ I didn't like it   ○ I hated it
2. Would you recommend this book to a friend? (Check one)   ⊘ Definitely yes
   ○ Probably yes   ○ Maybe   ○ Probably not   ○ Definitely not
3. Is this the first **Sweet Valley Twins** book you've read?   ○ Yes
   If not, how many have you read in total? _50_
   In the past month? (Check one)   ○ 1-2   ○ 3-4   ⊘ 5+
4. Would you read more **Sweet Valley Twins** books? (Check one)
   ⊘ Definitely yes   ○ Probably yes   ○ Maybe   ○ Probably not
   ○ Definitely not
5. Have you read any other **Sweet Valley** books? (Check all that apply)
   ⊘ Sweet Valley Kids   ⊘ The Unicorn Club   ○ Sweet Valley High
   ⊘ Sweet Valley University
   If yes, how many have you read in the past month? _10_
6. Did you get this book in the **Sweet Valley Best Friends Twin Pack**? (Check one)
   ⊘ Yes   ○ No
   If yes, where did you first learn about the **Sweet Valley Best Friends Twin Pack**?
   (Check one)   ○ Advertisement   ⊘ Store Display   ○ Friend
   ○ Other (Please specify)_____
7. Who picked out this book for you? (Check one)   ⊘ I did (reader)
   ○ Parents/Grandparents   ○ Friend   ○ Other (Please specify)
8. Where was this book bought?   ⊘ Bookstore   ○ Grocery Store
   ○ Drugstore   ○ Discount Chain Store (like K-Mart)
   ○ Other (Please specify) _____

Your Name_____
Address_____
City_____ State_____ Zip_____
Date of Birth_____/_____/_____

Please send this completed questionnaire to: Sweet Valley Twins, 1540 Broadway, BFYR Marketing, 20th floor, New York, NY 10036